SONG TITLE SERIES

ELTON JOHN

JOAN MAGUIRE

Copyright Page

National Library of Australia Cataloguing-in-Publication –
Publication entry

Creator:	Maguire, Joan, author
Title:	Elton John/ Joan Maguire.
Edition:	Large print edition.
ISBN:	9780994329776 (paperback)
Series:	Song title series (large print); book 12.
Notes:	Includes bibliography references
Subjects:	Detective and mystery stories
	Titles of musical compositions--Fiction

Dewey Number: A823. 4

Published with the assistance of CreateSpace and is available
through the Print on Demand network or
www.songtitleseries.com
This short story book was created and written
By Joan Maguire on April 5th 2013 ©
ISBN: 978-0-9941998-3-6
E-book re-written April 2014©
EIBSN: 978-0-9925964-8-4
This book was converted into large print in March 2015 ©
and is available through the same distributors as the normal
book or www.songtitleseries.com
ISBN: 978-0-9943297-7-6 (large print)

DEDICATION

I would like to dedicate this book and say to thank you to my Earth Angel David and his friends, who inspire and motivate me to achieve things that I never dreamt, were possible.

INTRODUCTION

Legally I cannot use Lyrics or Music because of Copyright but I can use song titles so in the creation of this book I have used 1776 song titles (Italicized) to make this futuristic story possible. Also due to the nature of my books; legally I must place a Reference (exactly as it is down loaded) and Bibliography after the story.

Earth is over populated so people are living on the moon and other surrounding planets but on one planet, a new type of criminal has started to try and manipulate the Universe by using a green mist that looks *just like strange rain* and his first target is women.

Two agents *Little Jeannie* and *Tiny Dancer* are helped to safety at the same time by a man with blue eyes; but how can he be in different parts of the Universe at the same time?

Find out how the women are affected and how does the agency solve the green mist mystery and capture the criminals

ACKNOWLEDGEMENTS

I would like to thank my daughters, Jenny and Kylie for their positive but critical input in the first draft of this book. With taking their input to mind, I have improved the book.

I would also like to thank my son Peter and his family for their support and help in keeping me grounded.

To my best friend Dawn, thank you for being there and supporting me. Somehow you always knew when I needed picking up with a good laugh.

I would like to thank Kay and Julie for their patience and understanding whilst teaching me and giving me the skills to present my unique books in the best way possible.

I would also like to thank Lloyd, Rita and Mark for helping me to put some authenticity to the Bacterial parts of this story

I would also like to thank everyone else who has helped me bring this book to life and to you for purchasing it.

DISCOVERING BOOKS

"*Bennie,* where are you?" shouted a frantic Pogo as he came rushing through the door into the reception area of Brumby and Sons Agency.

Pogo calm down. *Bennie and the Jets* are on their way to see the *Island girl* and *Lady D'Arbanville* on *Your Song.* Can I help you with anything?" asked *Nikita.*

Pogo replied "I wanted to see *Bennie* urgently because I have just had a report that the *Pinball Wizard* is on his way to visit *Lucy in the sky with diamonds* with the intention to steal some of them from her.

The report also states that he wants to enlist the aid of the *Mona Lisas and Mad Hatters* to kidnap and transport the king of Transvenus to the *madman across the water* because the *king must die* for some reason unknown at this moment."

"We have also had the report that *the king must die* given to us, but we don't know which king so *Tiny Dancer* is looking into it.

I am hoping that she would be able to verify the report by *tonight."* replied *Nikita.*

"*Tiny Dancer; they call her the cat,* don't they?" questioned Pogo.

"Yes, they do and it's because she can get into most places quite easily and quietly without being noticed; but then again you would think that someone would notice you; especially when you are six foot four inches tall, have *blue eyes* and blue hair and smells like *honey roll."* said Nikita.

"Not if you go the *club at the end of the street.* I think that nearly everyone in there looks like that; except that many of the patrons would be a bit shorter than *Tiny Dancer,* but not that much shorter. Even the *travelin' band, I'm Your Puppet,* fits in there.

They are a *way to blue* for me because they play the old style of black folk music with a slow tempo that sounds like *sad songs.* The music is great most of the time but too many *sad songs* can bring you down.

Saturday night is alright for fighting those sorts of *sad songs* but I prefer to be where there is a *whole lot of shakin' going on.* I love my faster music and I *wouldn't have it any other way.*

I also love to watch the *freak on the dance floor dancing in the end zone."* chuckled Pogo.

"*I guess that's why they call it the Blues* Club. You know, Pogo, sometimes *sad songs say so much* to people and the same can be said for just about all styles of music.

Just instrumental music can show so many emotions in it. That is why a *travelin' band* will occasionally play just an instrumental song or one where there are not many words but a few extra riffs going through it. To me, *I don't care* what sort of music is playing; I like listening to just about every type.

Four Moods Buckmaster are one of my favorite bands because they can do just that; they can play a great variety of music that can put you in *four moods* in just one night; however, they always leave their audiences in a high mood when they finish their shows. They never finish with *sad songs* like the *Ballad of a Well-Known Gun* or the *Blues for My Baby and Me*.

Your sister can't twist very well, but she can sure dance to a *love song* but *you're so static* when you are out on the dance floor. I saw you both in there last month but I was with some friends who were leaving so I couldn't come over to say hello or *goodbye*." replied *Nikita*

Tom Dick and Harry walked through the office door, straight past the reception desk and headed towards their offices. Harry had something in his hand and said "Tom, *I can't tell the bottom from the top*. Can you say which way is up?

Dick we'll catch up when you get back from *Your Song* and by then your own Accounting Agency office will have been refurbished and ready to move back into."

Tom stopped and looked back to the reception desk before saying "*I guess that's why they call it the Blues* Club, alright.

Now if you were talking to *Medley;* one of the Brown Dirt Cowboys, he would tell you; especially if they were in *Sacrifice,* that for the *Captain & me, for string quartet, Hijo Macho* is the one we prefer to listen to, but for an *orchestral finale,* the theatre on Transvenus is the place to go.

Saturday night's alright to go out and have a few drinks and to listen to music.

You know that *you gotta love someone* who follows a *travellin' band up around the bend* of the *Yellow River* or *come down in time* and cross the *bridge* from the Music Play *House* to the *Solar Prestige a Gammon* outdoor concert park just to listen to their music."

He then asked *Nikita* "Has Bennie gone to see *Lady D'Arbanville* yet?

I was listening to the *talking old soldiers* this morning and they enlightened me on what is happening on *Your Song* and if you think that *Bennie and the Jets* will be gone for the *best part of the day* and tomorrow; then think again. They may be gone for at least the next two weeks.

You can expect communication from *Daniel* advising you of this and he will give you an itinerary of where they will be going and what they will be doing."

"When *Tiny Dancer* returns could you please ask her to come to my office? Thank you." asked Harry, as he looked back around the corner.

He then called to Pogo " *Your sister can't twist but she can rock 'n' roll.* I was watching her last *Wednesday night* over at *Big Shot* while her *Rock and Roll Madonna* dance group went through their routines on the larger dance floor.

After they had finished their routine, I watched a couple of young children trying to copy one of their routines but because there were *no shoe strings on Louise*'s shoes she kept losing them.

In the end she took them off but her mother looked at her and said "And *who wears these shoes* for dancing?"

So Louise had to put her shoes back on to dance in."

"Well, it seems that I became frantic for nothing, so I'll be off. Velocity wanted to take me to see *Wasteland* at the movies this afternoon but I have already seen it and I wasn't really impressed with it.

It was reported to be a Science Fiction movie made at the *Goodbye Yellow Brick Road* Mansion down on Earth but I didn't think it was. I felt as if it was more of a poor *variation on Friends* of the Not So Cuddly Bears.

You know the movie where the young couple seems to *step into Christmas* by passing *through the storm* of the century and straight into the Teddy Bear's Picnic.

I'll let you know if I hear anymore news coming in from my sources." said Pogo.

"*I've seen that movie too;* in fact, I have seen both movies and like you, I wasn't really impressed. Both movies were tame compared with the *club at the end of the street. Tell me what the papers say* about it in the reviews when they come out. Oh, talking about papers; have you seen the latest articles in the *High Flying Bird Credits* Social Paper that states "*December will be magic again* if you go on the new crazy fad diet."

I bet it's one of those diets that came from Earth many years ago and didn't work.

If I hear anything that you should know or if we need you, will you be at your regular place?" asked *Nikita*.

"Yes, I will be." said Pogo as he left the office.

Rocket Man came in, passing Pogo who was on his way out, carrying a bag of *rotten peaches* and a few other items in brown bags, and asked for Harry.

At the very same instance, Harry called *Nikita* on the intercom and told her that he was expecting *Rocket Man* and would she please send him in as soon as he arrived.

Once in Harry's office and as he was sitting down on the high backed leather chair that he usually sat in, *Rocket Man* asked "What is so urgent that I have been summoned for?

I was on my way to *Your Song* when I got your message and I had to ask the hostess to *take me to the pilot* so that I could get him to change his course to land here. If I am flying and I have to change course, I always talk to the pilot personally so that nothing confidential can be overheard by the cabin staff or other passengers."

"I have had a communication from *Daniel* stating that he and *Bennie and the Jets* were on *Your Song* with *Lady D'Arbanville*.

Evidently she found the *Island girl* wandering in a trance like condition and saying over and over again "*Sorry seems to be the hardest word* to say, *Sorry seems to be the hardest word* to say."

This, and a report that the *Pinball Wizard* is on his way to visit *Lucy in the sky with diamonds* with the intention to steal some of them, and with the aid of the *Mona Lisas and Mad Hatters,* he also wants to kidnap and transport the King of Transvenus to the *madman across the water* because the *king must die* for some reason unknown at this moment. Tom has *Tiny Dancer* working on that report and she is to report in at any time.

She said that she would have to say *goodbye Yellow Brick Road* Jazz and Blues Club and miss *someone's final song* but *I guess that's why they call it the blues;* sometimes you have to leave before a good songs finished."

Nikita and Tom went bursting into Harry's office interrupting his conversation with *Rocket Man* with Tom saying "*Tiny Dancer* has been found in *Sacrifice* by St Peter.

It seems that she too was found wandering in a trance like condition saying "*Sorry seems to be the hardest word* to say in *Philadelphia Freedom. Sorry seems to be the hardest word* to say in *Philadelphia Freedom.*"

I have sent *Roy Rogers* to bring her back *to the Guesthouse* where we will get *Dixie Lily* to take her out into the *empty garden* to try and bring her out of the trance.

If we can get her out of the trance, then she might remember what happened to her and tell us who or what was responsible and it may also be a clue to what has happened to the *Island girl.*"

Nikita returned to her desk as *Rocket Man* blurted out "You have sent *Roy Rogers* to *Sacrifice* to bring her back in *Old 67.*

Louise could run and move faster than Roy could fly; even if there were *no shoestrings on Louise's* shoes and they kept coming off.

You are then going to get *Dixie Lily,* that *dirty little girl,* to try and bring her out of the trance in the *empty garden.* Are you mad, you should have sent me to get her?"

Harry said "Now settle down *Rocket Man,* we have a more important mission for you to go on. Don't worry about *Tiny Dancer;* she'll be alright.

That *dirty little girl,* Dixie Lily, was once one of the *street kids* until we found out that she has *healing hands* and that her *heart in the right place.*

She was offered employment with our agency and a place of her own to live.

When she accepted, we gave her all that she needed and we have offered to brighten up the *empty garden* for her but she has refused by telling us that it is easier to heal people in an *empty garden*.

Roy Rogers may not be the most ideal person for us to have sent but he will bring *Tiny Dancer* back safely and he knows so many people who will help him along the way.

Now; as for your mission, we want you to go to *Crocodile Rock* and find out all you can about this *madman across the water*. Also, see if you can find out which *king must die* and try to prevent it.

Now as *Saturday night is alright for fighting* and a lot of that happens there, please don't get involved as it could blow your assignment.

Crocodile Rock can be a cold place and it is even *too low for zero in the summertime*. Some people also say that it can be as *cold as Christmas in the middle of the year,* so do you have something warmer to wear whist you're there?" asked Harry.

"Yes." replied *Rocket Man* "I have *my strongest suit* that was especially *made for me* and *made in England* plus it is very warm. How do you want me to travel to *Crocodile Rock?"*

Tom replied "I think that it would be best for you to board the *Skyline Pigeon* Intercity Shuttle craft as one of the normal *passengers* travelling on holiday *in the summertime*. It will be less likely that you will be noticed when you get there.

Once you are free of the airport, go to the *Circle Of Life Cookie Factory* and the *sweet painted lady* will say "*Take a walk with me."* and you will reply "What, through all the *sugar on the floor."*

She will then tell you where to *meet Christine* who is expecting you and will help you. Now you had better get moving as the craft leaves in three hours."

A few more details were discussed between the three men before Harry and Tom were finally on their own.

Harry pulled out a bottle of *Elderberry Wine* and said to Tom "I feel as if I am jumping *into the old man's shoes* again, just like I did a few months ago while dad was away.

Do you want a glass of wine or a *Durban Deep* Scotch?"

Tom had just poured himself a scotch when through the intercom on Harry's desk *Nikita* said "Harry, *Captain Fantastic and the Brown Dirt Cowboys* need to talk to you immediately. They are calling you from *Levon.*"

Harry looked at Tom and said surprisingly "*Levon;* what the heck are they doing in *Levon.* They were supposed to be heading for *Amoreena,* on the *bad side of the Moon.*"

Again through the intercom on his desk *Nikita* said "Harry. *Dan Dare* and *Little Jeanie* have *come together* in *Harmony* and need to talk to you immediately by *satellite* but it seems that I have lost contact with both parties.

Shall I try to get them back?"

Harry exclaimed "What is going on

here! *Dan Dare; pilot of the future* is supposed to be training in *Muse*. *Little Jeanie* is supposed to be undercover as the *part time love* of *Cartier* on Urallas. All we need now is to hear from *Carla Etude* who should be in *Cotton Fields* on Earth."

Again through the intercom on his desk *Nikita* said "Harry, *Carla Etude* needs to talk to you immediately by satellite but the connection is breaking up."

Tom finished his drink and as he was pouring another one he said "Yes, I'd like to know too. All our people are not where they're supposed to be; they're all scattered all over the Universe.

Do we have an *Indian Sunset* today with the *Stormbringer* spreading *all the nasties* like a *theme from a non-existent TV series?*

I wonder if the *Spirit in the sky* is confused as well.

I am glad that it's you who is jumping *into the old man's shoes*. I don't think that I would be able to handle this mess on my own.

If it gets too much for you, just *yell help* and I'll come and give you a hand." Harry looked at Tom and said "Guess what brother; if you think that it's going to be *like father, like son,* then we are both going to be jumping *into the old man's shoes* together.

It's getting late and it will be difficult to contact our people now, so I suggest that we both get in here first thing in the morning and start contacting everybody and find out what the heck is going on.

I'm going home now and don't forget to *turn the lights out when you leave*. Good night."

Nikita and Harry left at the same time.

Nikita said good night and walked through the building's door onto the street and had only taken a few steps when she suddenly went into a trance like state and started saying "*Sorry seems to be the hardest word* to say in *Philadelphia Freedom* because *Saturday night's alright for fighting* as the *bitch is back*. *Sorry seems to be the hardest word* to say in *Philadelphia Freedom* because

Saturday night's alright for fighting as the *bitch is back."*

Harry rushed outside and pulled *Nikita* back into the building and then using the security phone, called Tom down to the Foyer.

Tom left the elevator and as he approached, Harry said "I noticed a pale green mist before I walked out the door, so I stopped to observe it and it was *just like strange rain* falling. *Nikita* walked out into it and immediately went into the trance like state and started saying over and over again *"Sorry seems to be the hardest word* to say in *Philadelphia Freedom* because *Saturday night's alright for fighting* as the *bitch is back. Sorry seems to be the hardest word* to say in *Philadelphia Freedom* because *Saturday night's alright for fighting* as the *bitch is back."*

There were other people outside walking past as they normally would but they didn't seem to be affected. I wonder who she means when she says "The *bitch is back?"*

I also think that we should spend the night here and not take any chances in venturing outside until we can find out more about this mist and why it only affects some people."

"I guess you're right." said Tom "how are we going to find out what's going on and who can we ask?

I'm glad that you were still in the building when you noticed the mist; you could have been *driving home, driving to Jack's place* or *driving to Universal* Heights to check on dad's place. Who knows what would have happened if you were out in it and it affected you like it has Nikita."

"I only wish that we could contact dad. I am pretty certain that he would know. He had to deal with many *strangers* and strange happenings before he retired. It will only be four more days before he gets back so we had better do the best we can until then." replied Harry.

"I suppose if we are going to stay here, we would be better off back in our offices or in the Boardroom.

What are we going to do about Miss Repeat here? If she keeps going on and on, I'm likely to get a bit annoyed and do something to the *poor cow.*

Now *where's the Shoorah* that dad kept here for when we played up when we were kids?" said Tom.

"I'll take *Nikita* to the Boardroom and you go to her room and get the rest of her personal belongings, then get our personal belongings and I'll meet you up there.

Whatever you do; don't go near an open window or open one up. The last thing I need is for you to end up like *Nikita."* said Harry.

Tom took about half an hour before he reached the Boardroom where his brother and Nikita were.

Nikita was lying on a couch and just before she became silent she said "*Sorry seems to be the har...*"

"What took you so long?" shouted Harry "this woman was driving me crazy with her continuous babbling so I gave her a sedative to shut her up.

Don't worry it's a very mild one and she will only sleep for a few hours at the most so we had better sit and try to figure out what we're going to do and who we should contact first.

What's that book you have under your arm?"

"Oh, this." said Tom as he took a very old looking book out from under his arm "I found this in Nikita's room. It looks like some sort of book archival system for back in dad's early days. I had a quick look at it and thought it might be helpful to us as it says that all the archives are store in the back room off the Boardroom. We might find a solution or some helpful information in there."

"Well brother. It seems that I am not the only one who thinks outside the square around here. *You get brighter* as you are getting older but you should do it more often because when you do, you come up with some great ideas.

Now let's have a look in that book?" remarked Harry.

They both grabbed a drink and sat

down at the small table and started to read the book.

After they had gone nearly half way through the book, Tom saw an entry that seemed to jog his childhood memory of a story about a natural *sinner* who spent three weeks in the *Goodbye Yellow Brick Road* Mansion on Earth that his father used to like telling him.

"Look at this entry!" exclaimed Tom "It's about one of dad's stories that he used to tell us on the occasional *Wednesday night* when he was home.

I remember it well and if my memory serves me right, then we would find some information there that might just give us a start in solving our dilemma or have *you got another thought* on where to start?"

"No, not yet." replied Harry "so let's go to the other room and see if we can find this book. Nikita will be fine to be left on her own. It looks like we're about to say *good morning to the night* and working right through it so *whenever you're ready,* we'll get started."

The brothers were surprised by the amount of books that were in the room. Some of the books seemed to be that old that they must have belonged to their grandfather or even to his father. In one particular cabinet, there seemed to be a collection of completely different books altogether from the other similarly bound books.

Tom looked at some of the titles which amazed him and the books *Elton's New York Stories, Ballad Of Dan Bailey (1909 - 34),* The *Gods Love Nubia* and *Solar Prestige A Gammon* caught his eye.

As he took the book *Ballad Of Dan Bailey (1909 -34)* from the shelf, he noticed three sheets of music wedged between two of the other books, so he took them out to look at them.

One sheet was named *Elton's song* and was signed "To *dear John.*" but the signature had faded. There were two copies of *Hymn 2000*.

One copy of *Hymn 2000* had "The marriage of the *Honky Cat Daniel* and the *Honky Cat Chloe Chameleon.*

The poor man now wears a *ball and chain.*" written on it and the other copy had "*Michelle's song.* Sorry darling, *mama can't buy you love.*"

There was also some *love letters* and a smaller different covered book tied together with string.

The *writing* seemed very familiar to him and he tried to recall where he had seen it before as he stared at the words "*January; Love her like me* and please *don't go breaking my heart* and please, please *don't let the sun go down on me* like you let it go down on...*" he couldn't make out the last name because it had been smudged many years ago.

He pulled them off the shelf and put them in his pocket to read later.

"Hey Tom, I think that I've found something in these books. Let's take them back into the other room and read through them because *it's getting dark in here* and I need more light." shouted an excited Harry.

READING BOOKS

This time the boys grabbed a couple of bottles of *Elderberry Wine* before sitting down to read the books.

"Listen to this." said Tom "I think this must be just after our great grandfather started the business. Back in 1929, Danny Bailey had just got himself engaged to a female named Madonna. She was also known as *rock and roll Madonna* due to her love of dancing.

One evening while she was teaching a group of *Mona Lisas and Mad Hatters* a special dance routine, a *cocaine* addict entered the hall and went around attacking the females in the dance group with an iron bar.

Madonna stepped in to try and stop him but he turned on her instead and hit her continuously all over her body and head, leaving her with many broken bones, cuts, bruises and just barely alive.

The male dancers were unable to pull the addict away from Madonna until a few moments later and once they had, the addict was able to break free from their clutches and ran out the hall door, disappearing into the darkness of *Grey Seal* Street.

Madonna was taken to hospital but there was not much they could do for her. All the doctors believed that she would be *better off dead* because of her injuries; she would never have any sort of life again and she would never wear her *eight hundred dollar shoes* for dancing again.

Danny Bailey went berserk after hearing the news and of the *madness* that had happened that day and went looking for the *ugly* person, as he was called, who could do such a thing.

Danny Bailey finally caught up with the *ugly* person *up around the bend* of the *Yellow River,* just outside the *one horse town* of *Latitude*.

When the *angry young man* was asked why did he attack the females, especially Madonna, the *ugly* man said "My name is Rudolph and I am in love with *Pinky,* one of the dancers, but *when a woman doesn't want you* because you can't dance like she can, what can you do?

My love for *Pinky* was like *my elusive drug* and getting Pinky to love me became an obsession to me. I became very frustrated and depressed that all my efforts to win Pinky were not working so I contacted a friend of mine, *Stinker,* in the *Sick City Retreat* who got me some stuff from *Razor Face.*

I didn't realize that the stuff, cocaine, could alter your mind so much that it can make you a *slave* to your emotions.

Although *it's still rock and roll to me,* it's still only a dance and Madonna and the others should not have gotten in my way. *Rock 'n' roll Madonna* was helping to drive *Pinky* further away from me so I thought the only way to get my girl back was to take *rock 'n' roll Madonna* out of the picture for a while.

I never went in there to kill anybody but if I broke a leg or arm, then they wouldn't be able to dance for a couple of months."

It is written here that Danny Bailey told

Rudolph "A *scared man can't gamble* anymore with other people's lives. *Rock and roll Madonna* and I were to be married in a couple of months' time. The doctors are now saying that she would be *better off dead* because of the injuries that you inflicted on her.

And as for some of the other females; well, two of them are in a critical but stable condition in hospital, *Sarah escapes* with severe bruising and Pinky has not got a scratch on her; however, she is helping the *legal boys* with their investigations and hoping that they find you before I do.

I'm still standing and so are you but Madonna will never stand again even if she does survive her injuries so now all I can say to you is that you had better *run Rudolph run* and send a *telegraph to the afterlife* to tell them that you're on your way, because *I feel like a bullet* or two is going to draw your final *curtains* once I can get *my father's gun* out of this *shoulder holster.*"

The next entry on that subject says

that before Danny Bailey died in 1934, he set up the *Rock and Roll Madonna* Dance Academy in honour of the only love of his life and "It's *sixty years on* since I have thought of my very dear friend Dan.

If you had not done what you did, then I would have given you a partnership in my business and *my father's gun* for coming in with me.

You always said "*Don't let the sun go down on me.*" but now I have no control over it. Some days I still feel as if I'm *sleeping with the past* because I *miss you* and your company more than anyone would know.

Not even my dear wife, *Susie* knows how I feel. I'm glad that Pinky wrote the *Ballad of Danny Bailey (1909 – 34)* and placed it on your tombstone along with the anonymous *Ballad of a Well-known Gun* that we both know was written by me."

Harry turned back a few pages in the book that he was reading and said "This book must have been written many years later in our grandfather's era.

It says here that the government of the day has just started exploring space to find out if there are any other planets besides Earth, the Moon, *Your Song* or Little *Your Song*ulis and Urallas that can sustain our life form.

We know that there are other species of life forms out there that are similar to ours like the *Neanderthal Man* and the *Fascist Faces* who are becoming helpful and friendly as they learn about us and we about them.

The main party of the *Neanderthal Man* that we seem to engage are the ones *between seventeen and twenty*. They must act as the ambassadors for their elders. I think that the Fascist Faces would be as untrustworthy as a *candle in the wind;* they could either leave us alone or cause a lot of trouble.

It also states here that as the *pilot* of *The Cage* Space Craft was nearing a planet called *Salvation One,* he noticed a pale green mist that looked *just like strange rain* so he took a photo of it before he turned away from that sector.

They don't know how, but some of the mist must have gotten into the craft's ventilation system because for about three hours after turning away from the mist, the females in the crew went into a trance and started saying "*Sorry seems to be the hardest word* to say so *I guess that's why they call it the blues. Sorry seems to be the hardest word* to say so *I guess that's why they call it the blues.*"

The male crew members seemed to be unaffected. The medic on board the space craft put most of the women to sleep but monitored two others, who were kept awake, in the sick bay.

The ones who were put to sleep, woke up three hours later with amnesia of what they had just experienced but the other two in the sick bay did not come out of the trance and once back on the Moon, they were taken to the *Western Ford Gateway* Observation Station just in case they did come out of the trance with medical issues.

The following day, one female crew member did come out of the trance without any issues but the other one developed a *multiple personality* disorder a year later due to the trauma that she went through.

For granddad to know that, I think that he must have had a person working on the inside of the station, who was able to give him that information. *Western For Gateway* Observation Station was a cover for a secret medical facility for any of the space crew personnel who experienced any out of the normal issues on their flights.

Once *The Cage* Space Craft had re-landed and the door was opened, other medical teams entered and the leader of the medical team said "Before anyone leaves, I must find out what happened. *Take me to the pilot* please."

The medical leader came out of *the bridge* with the pilot and the navigator saying "Your right, the *camera never lies*.

It definitely does look like pale green rain; however, it is so pale that another person wouldn't see the real color.

There will also be some samples taken from the outside of your craft to see if any rain has remained on it so that we can do some experiments and tests on them. I would like the rest of the crew, especially the men to have a medical check and bloods taken as soon as your debriefing has finished.

That's all captain."

"Well, does it say anything about whether samples were taken and what the results from them were?" enquired Tom.

"No." said Harry "But here is another report on the green rain.

This one comes from Urallas, that's on the other side of the universe, twenty years later.

It states that two young boys were sitting on their parent's *porch swing in Tupelo* when the green rain passed over them and they began laughing hysterically and humming a tune.

When the boy's parents went to find out what was so funny and why they were humming, the boys told their parents between bouts of laughter "A green rain fell on us and we started humming but we don't know what it is because *this song has no title.*" and then they started laughing again.

Two days later, the boys were still *wide eyed and laughing,* so their mother took them to their medical centre.

I suspect that tests were done on the boys but there is no report written here, and there's no other entry about them either.

Have you got anything to eat in your office? I have a couple of tins of *Curtains* Real Ham in the white and green *Tinderbox* that I was saving to *step into Christmas* Eve with. *Ain't nothing like the real thing* to eat when you *step into Christmas.*

I'm starting to get hungry and I suspect that when Nikita wakes up, she'll be hungry as well. She will also want an explanation on what happened to her. I am hoping that she will come around like the other women we have read about have.

Understanding women is hard at the best of times but I have no idea what would have gone on inside her head caused by the green rain.

A *woman's needs* and tastes are different from ours so I hope that we can supply her with food that she won't moan over for the rest of the week because that is something I don't need in *my life* right now and neither do you."

"I have three tins of *Rotten Peaches* for *Rocket Man, Honey Roll,* a packet of Lemon *Bitter Fingers,* a couple of tins of *Aquarium John* Sandwich Meat and Fish and a few cooked *Jamaica Jerk Off* or *Jack Rabbit* pies in the *li'l 'frigerator.* We can heat the pies quite easily." replied Tom.

"Getting *back to the Aquarium* John, do you have any that doesn't taste like *hay chewed* and then put in sauce? I don't *live like horses* so I won't eat like them." asked Harry.

"What do you mean by "*It's hay chewed* and then put in sauce?" said Tom "most of the tins I have contain either fish or *birds* like chicken, turkey or duck. I don't like red meat in tins so I won't buy it.

The *Jamaica Jerk Off* pie is my favorite because they contain a mixture of beef, lamb and *snake in the grass* so I am going to have at least one of them.

We still haven't thought about what we are going to do next.

Everyone wants us to contact them urgently and what if Nikita comes out of the trance and is unable to work. We will be flat out doing our own jobs at that time, let alone doing her job as well.

If she does come out of the trance and is able to work, will she be able to take the stress of what is required of her at this time. If she doesn't come out of the trance; what can we do with her or where can we send her, home, not on her own we can't."

"As we have had to get *into the old man's shoes* together over this situation, why don't we start thinking like the old man would?

What would he do first? Who would he contact to take care of Nikita if she needed to be looked after?" asked Harry.

"Mmm, I think that the old man would contact *Bennie and The Jets* first and get them to send *Daniel* back here.

I know that dad would contact that *dirty little girl*, what's her name....Oh yes, Dixie Lily to look after Nikita in the *empty garden*, even though she is expecting *Tiny Dancer* at any time.

The old man would then contact each of the other people working out in the field, *one* at a time and set up a conference call time so that we can all talk out each issue at hand.

Dad always did say that *united we stand* and if the urgency turns out to have something to do with the green rain then we would have to try and work out a solution that is acceptable to all of us. Even if it means that it is only a temporary solution to start with." said Tom.

"Very good." said Harry "That is exactly what we'll do first thing in the morning.

Now I think that it's time to eat and then we'll try and get some sleep.

I'll have a *Jack Rabbit* pie heated to start off with and then I'll have some *Honey Roll* and a couple of Lemon *Bitter Fingers*. I won't have too much because we may need something for breakfast in the morning."

"I'll have one of those and a *cold* drink as well." mumbled a sleepy sounding Nikita "it's about time you waited on me for a change.

What happened and am I in the Boardroom at work?

I meant to do my work today and then go home to sleep and come back here tomorrow; not go to sleep and wake up still at work."

Harry told Tom to go and get the food and some drinks and then he turned to Nikita and asked "Nikita, how are you?

Just sit there and I'll explain what has been going on. This afternoon as we were leaving, I noticed some pale green mist outside the building and it was just like strange rain and before I could stop you, you walked out the door straight into it.

You immediately went into a trance like state and started saying "*Sorry seems to be the hardest word* to say in *Philadelphia Freedom* because *Saturday night's alright for fighting* as the *bitch is back. Sorry seems to be the hardest word* to say in *Philadelphia Freedom* because *Saturday night's alright for fighting* as the *bitch is back.*"

I rushed outside and pulled you back into the foyer and then I called Tom down.

Neither of us was sure of what to do next so we decided to stay here the night in the Boardroom. *Sorry,* but I gave you a mild tranquilizer to knock you out because you were driving us crazy with your constant repeating.

I had Tom go to your room and bring your other personal belongings up here for safe keeping and whilst he was down there, he found this old book.

He started reading it and he became familiar with one of the entries that told us about these other books. I wasn't even aware of the back room and it *amazes me* that no one has ever mentioned these books before and of their whereabouts.

Tom was reading one that we think was from our great, great grandfather's era. The more I read of the times around my grandfather's era, the more I was learning about this green mist but I still don't know enough on what affects it can have on a person so I would be happy if you would spend the night here with us because we can keep an eye on you in case you suffer any reactions to it.

First thing tomorrow morning, we are going to call all our other people who are out in the field, starting with *Bennie and the Jets* and then the others *one* by *one* and try and set up a conference call time so we all can work on the issues at hand. Tom feels that it may have something to do with this green mist.

Now if you are up to it, we could certainly use your help. We are also going to see if *Daniel* can come back here for a short period to help us out.

Now, what do you say about that?"

"Well, *someone saved my life tonight...* Ah! Food, I'm starved." said Nikita, looking past Harry to an opening door. "Now as for your other plans, I think they should be alright. Having *Daniel* here to help out, will be rewarding and interesting, because he has an unusual and unique way of doing things.

I know that he has been with the agency for many, many years and when I have asked him how long, he just looks at me with those beautiful *blue eyes,* smiles and then says "Look for the *answer in the sky."* Do you know how long he has been with your agency? I have looked in the staff records because I do the pays but I can't find his actual starting date.

How are you going to know if it's safe for us to go outside tomorrow? You do know that we will have to go to our homes at least to shower and change our clothes."

"We were going to work that out after

we have spoken to everybody tomorrow. Those books in the back room; did you know about them?" asked Tom and pulled the small book and letters out of his pocket and placed them on the table.

Nikita finished swallowing her mouthful of drink and answered "Yes, I was aware of the books and the room but I have never been in there. The only time that I have been up here, is when your father called me in to take the minutes for a special meeting that he had with Mr. *En Sus Ojos* two days after I started working here.

The old book that you found in my room was there when I started and when I asked your father about it, he told me that it was a catalogue for the books in the back room of the Boardroom and could I please keep it safe and make another copy for him. I made the copy of the book and gave it to him and we spoke no more about it. In fact, I had forgotten all about that book until now."

As Harry was eating, he was reading at the same time. "No, I don't *believe* it.

It couldn't be the same person." said Harry.

In unison both Tom and Nikita said "What is it? What have you read now?"

Harry said "Listen to this entry "*The bitch is back* in *Belfast* and I *believe* that I am going to have to deal with her because *Daniel* is with St Peter trying to find out who tried to *burn down the mission* in *Phoenix.*"

I really don't think that the *Daniel* mentioned here in granddad's journal could be the same *Daniel* who worked with dad and now us.

Our *Daniel* doesn't look old enough to have even worked for all those years with dad, let alone granddad. It must be a coincidence that they both do the same work and have the same name."

He then continued to read out loud "Who would think that the bitch could be *young gifted and black?* I remember the first time we met and she said "*Don't let the sun go down on me* because I despise the *Midnight Creeper.* He will *come down in time* and blow out the *candle in the wind* leaving me with a head full of *sad songs* to get me through the night.

Tonight you will have to catch *one* of the planes to *Reverie* and then the train to *Logos* and walk back from there to the *Cottonfields Country Comfort* Motel, because the driver will tell you that *this train don't stop there anymore.*

You will be glad to say "*goodbye Yellow Brick Road.*" once you have reached the motel because you'll hear nothing but *whispers* coming from the trees whilst you're walking and the trees won't be whispering about the *love of the common people* either."

That afternoon before I left, she slipped a small package into my hand and told me to put it straight into my inside jacket pocket and not to take it out until the following morning once the sun had completely risen.

Then she looked at me strangely and quietly said "*We all fall in love sometimes* but *don't go breaking my heart* because *it's me that you need* to keep you floating down *the river of dreams. It's all in the game* but it's *easier to walk away* from a *man who never died* than it is living in *Jimmie Rodger's Dream.*

Yes, *I've seen that movie too* and *I've seen the saucers* in the *heels of the wind* and I know who travels with their occupants beside the *captain & the kid....* the man with the *blue eyes* and *everybody gonna* know when he is around."

She turned and walked towards the Ladies Room and that was the last time I saw her. I never got to ask her to explain herself so I didn't know what the meaning was to what she had said.

The following day I opened the parcel to find a note which read "*White lady White powder,* not *young gifted and black.* When you bought me my last drink, if you had looked, you would have seen that I have *blue eyes* not brown or black.

Can you feel the love tonight? I want love especially as *my baby loves lovin'* so *don't go breaking my heart* and *don't let*

49

the sun go down on me because *I don't wanna go on with you like that.*

If you want my magic and *part time love* then *come and get it,* if not I will be another *victim of love* and do the *walk of shame* down the *cold highway* until another comes along.

If the river can bend; then so can I. *I'm still standing* tall and I will say *good morning freedom* again and *don't let the sun go down on me* again until I am somewhere safe and warm."

The parcel itself was a box with white powder in it and it was then that I realized that *she sold me magic* and it would be with me always. It was something that I could use at any time to save my life or just relax with.

There were also some small *postcards from Richard Nixon* in England, on Earth, with a very pale green rain falling behind him, a small Christmas card in which was written "*Merry Christmas Maggie Thatcher.*" and a sealed envelope with "*Happy Birthday Elton.*" written on it.

I held the envelope up to the light and

I could see that it was empty.

I have no idea why she gave me those things but I have kept them just in case I run into her again and then I can give them back. Maybe she might even explain what she said to me.

Later that morning, I was sitting in the motel's bar when a man came in wearing a *monkey suit* minus the head. He walked up to a waitress and whilst showing her the timetable asked "You have a station here, so if *this train don't stop there anymore,* where can we catch it?

We can't walk too far as there are *no shoe strings on Louise'*s shoes and they come off when she walks, besides she is too big and heavy for me to carry for a long distance.

We are trying to *return to Paradise* by the end of the month because we want to *step into Christmas* at home with our families.

There is a *spotlight on Christmas* this year because Louise is expecting our first child and we would like it to be a *merry Christmas baby.*

The stranger with *blue eyes* and long blonde hair, who was looking at that *man* through the window, and he pointed to me, told Louise that we should not *go it alone* in having the baby but we should try to get home to our families before the pale green mist comes through *this town tonight*.

If we can catch the train we will be far away from here by *tonight*. He also told her, that if we see any other people along our travels that we should warn them about the green mist and tell them to stay under cover until the sun has completely risen in the morning when it will be safe to venture outside again."

The waitress replied "Thank you for the warning for *tonight*. There is a bus that will pass through here in an hour but that will go *all the way down to El Paso* which is in the opposite direction to where you want to go.

You can wait for it and catch it in front of the *Sartorial Eloquence* Fragrance Store, two blocks down from here."

As the man in the monkey suit turned

to leave, another younger man walked through the door with his raised arm in the air and shouted "*Who wears these shoes?* They were sitting outside the door and if whoever doesn't want to lose them, then they should put them back on their feet."

The monkey suited man replied worriedly "They belong to my wife. Because there are *no shoe strings on Louise's* shoes, she tends to lose them when she is walking. My wife was wearing them just a few minutes ago. Didn't you see her outside anywhere?"

The younger man replied "No. I didn't see anyone; however, I didn't really take a good look around."

A woman's voice was heard saying "They are my shoes. I took them off because my feet were tired and sore. May I have them back please?

Sials, if we are going to catch the bus that the stranger came back and told me about, then, let us please go now, but if we are going to wait until tomorrow, then let us find a room for the night.

I don't wanna go on with you like that; you need to shower or least change into some normal clothes."

Tom said "Maybe we will be safe to leave the building and venture outside sometime tomorrow morning after the sun has fully risen. Nikita you might even be able to say *good morning freedom* if the green mist has passed.

A few times, the statement "*The bitch is back.*" have been mentioned but no one has identified who she is or where she's from.

Harry, I'm going to turn in for the night; don't you stay awake all night reading because we are going to need your alert brain tomorrow as well."

Nikita picked up the book tied with the letters and untied the string and as she started reading it, she said "I'm not tired at the moment so reading this book might help me get to sleep although *it ain't gonna be easy* seeing I was sedated late this afternoon. *It's me that you need* bright eyed and ready to go in the morning.

Someone saved my life tonight by bringing me back into the building and sedating me. Who knows what may have happened to me otherwise, so thank you."

Nikita opened the book and was surprised to see that it was a diary that seemed to be written by a female.

She read "Today is the day when I will change the rest of my life. I will have a *dream come true* when I marry Arthur. No longer will he have to say each night "*Goodbye Yellow Brick Road* house, I will see you tomorrow."

Today, he will *give me the love* that will never be like a *candle in the wind,* it will be *the one* that will last for the rest of our lives.

We will make our promises to each other with the *Spirit in the sky* as our witness, he will put the ring on my finger and he will *kiss the bride*.

I was told once that your *mama can't buy you love* and I'm sure that she would never had been able to buy the love that Arthur is giving me because it is just so special, real and true.

It's a pity that we had to change our wedding place from inside the mission to the *empty garden* beside it, but someone tried to *burn down the mission* so the *empty garden* has been turned into an outdoor chapel.

Lord, please *don't let the sun go down on me* until our service is over and then it will be *wonderful tonight* as our love will also be *written in the stars*.

My baby loves lovin' and that is what I will give him for the rest of my life. I pray that there will be a *Honky cat* or two wandering through our garden when we say our vows, as it is believed that they are the luckiest cats to be around and I *believe* that too.

Hopefully in *sixty years on* from now I will be able to *look back* and *know why I'm in love* with Arthur still and he will still be in love with me. We will live a *simple life* and I hope that we will be *blessed* with children. I will also help him build up his business but then only our Lord knows what *lies* ahead for us."

Nikita wanted to read more of the diary but she knew that trying to find answers to the current issues had to come first, so she put that one down and began reading one of the other books.

THE RESCUE

Nikita was aware that Harry was still awake but became so engrossed in the book that she was reading that she wasn't really listening to the voice that she heard talking to her.

After a few seconds, she put her book down and said "Harry, would you please repeat what you just said because I never heard it all clearly?"

Harry looked up from his book and over to Nikita and replied "I didn't say anything to you." and they both looked at Tom, who was fast asleep.

"Didn't you just tell me that *out of the blue,* I will have to take a shuttle but I won't have to ask the crew to *take me to the pilot,* because the day after *New Year's Day* I will have to attend a meeting at the *Seasons Reprise* Conference Centre on *Your Song* with the *Island girl, Lady D'Arbanville and Lady Samantha?*

Then I will have to go *2000 miles* to *Border Song* on Mandalay and meet a *big man in a little suit* who will give me a letter from Amneris.

I will then have to deliver *Amneris'
letter* to the *man with all the toys* at the
North Pole on Earth and tell him that I
am only a *messenger* and he has to start
visiting *Mandalay again* thus preventing
an *act of war* from the children being
declared.

I will then visit our *friends, Rocket Man*
and *Tiny Dancer* in *Levon* and not to
forget that I *gotta get a meal ticket* each
time I want to eat out.

Rocket Man will then take me to St
Peter who will then escort me to *Val-Hala*
where I will find *warm love in a cold
world*.

Then you said something about *you
can make history, religion rehearsals,
recover your soul* and *written in the stars*
that I didn't hear properly." enquired
Nikita.

"No, I never spoke to you at all and we
know that Tom didn't say anything. You
may have thought you heard me talking
to you but it may just be a delayed
reaction to what happened to you today.

I think that I'll turn in now. Will you be alright if I do?" asked Harry.

"Yes, I'll be alright. Good night." said Nikita.

Surprisingly, even though Nikita didn't get any more sleep during the night, she was very much awake and was eager to go in the morning.

There was pot of hot coffee, a *Jack Rabbit* pie, a *Jamaica Jerk Off* pie, both hot, some slices of *Curtains* Real Ham and some fresh fruit, that she had down in her room, waiting for the boys when they woke up.

Both Tom and Harry enquired how she was and if she would be able to get through the day and Nikita replied "I am really raring to go. I feel so rested and relaxed that you would think that I had just come back from a long vacation in *Border Song*.

Those books are so fascinating and I read all night although *I swear I heard the night talkin'* to me again and this time I listened.

Now is not the time to discuss that, so

while you are eating your breakfast ,I am going to start contacting our other people starting with *Benny & the Jets*. *Daniel* usually answers the communications and transfers them to *Bennie* wherever he is. I will get *Rocket Man* and *Tiny Dancer* on the monitor, with *Dan Dare* and *Little Jeanie* and *Carla Etude;* I should be able to get through to them on satellite but as to getting communication through to *Captain Fantastic and the Brown Dirt Cowboys* will depend on whether they are still in *Levon*.

It will be much harder to contact them if they are on their way to or are in *Amoreena* on the *bad side of the moon*.

While I was heating your breakfast, I switched all communications over to the Boardroom. I think it would be to everyone's advantage if we could *come together* and work in a close proximity to each other today."

Nikita was just about to contact *Benny and the Jets* when *Daniel* contacted the office first.

"Good morning Nikita and how are you

this morning. You were not out in the mist long enough for it to have any real effects on you.

Before you put me through to Harry, I need you to turn to five, five *one* on your monitors and sets. This will make it easier for you to get communications through to everyone including *Captain Fantastic and the Brown Dirt Cowboys,* even if they are in *Amoreena on the bad side of the moon."* said Daniel.

Nikita questioningly asked "How do you know what happened to me yesterday? We haven't been in contact with anyone yet."

Daniel replied "A *Spirit in the sky* told me about you and that Tom and Harry have found the old books in the back room. Tell Harry that Bennie is here now and wants to talk with him."

"Harry." said Bennie "I think that *the bitch is back* and has teamed up with the *Midnight Creeper* so that they can kill a king. Which king and from what kingdom we have yet to find out.

Someone has found a way to

manipulate a pale green mist so that it causes different reactions to different people all over the universe. We also think that the *Pinball Wizard* could also be involved in the plot somewhere.

Lady D'Arbanville found the *Island girl, Emily,* just walking around in a trance like state saying "*Sorry seems to be the hardest word* to say so *I guess that's why they call it the blues. Sorry seems to be the hardest word* to say so *I guess that's why they call it the blues.*" and brought her back to the *White Room* wing of her estate.

Lady Samantha informed her parents who immediately came and gave her some sort of white powder that put her to sleep and she has only just woken up. *I'm still standing* outside her room because we haven't had a chance to ask her what happened but I will keep you informed.

An outbreak similar to this happened many years ago when your father had just started in the agency. It has worked out to be *sixty years on* since the outbreak before this one.

If this is anything like the last time and the *Pinball Wizard* is involved, he will do everything he can and will be laughing while he is *tearing us apart* as we try to sort out what is going on and how to deal with it.

I only wish that your father was back from his vacation because he would know what to do. I know that he used to write in a journal about everything that happened but I wouldn't know where he kept it. Have you had any contact with our other people?"

Harry replied "Dad was not the only one to keep journals about everything. Last night Tom and I found a room full of books dating back to our great, great grandfather's era. We have been reading the books to see if we can find out if what is happening now has happened before and if so, how was it cleared up.

Both Tom and I have had to jump *into the old man's shoes* to be able to work on this issue as it has affected us back here in the office as well.

Yesterday afternoon, Nikita and I were leaving for the day and as she stepped outside the building, she walked straight into a pale green mist and went into a trance like state and repeatedly kept saying "*Sorry seems to be the hardest word* to say in *Philadelphia Freedom* because *Saturday night's alright for fighting* as the *bitch is back. Sorry seems to be the hardest word* to say in *Philadelphia Freedom* because *Saturday night's alright for fighting* as the *bitch is back.*"

She was driving me that crazy that I gave her a sedative to make her sleep so that she would shut up and she seemed to have woken up alright.

We are going to get in contact with all our other people in the field now, who are scattered all over the universe and are not where they're supposed to be.

They all contacted us late yesterday afternoon asking us to contact them urgently but before we could get back to you and them, we lost all of our communications as you well know.

Now there are a couple of things that I would like to ask you; one, would you be able to spare *Daniel* for a few weeks or until we have sorted out this issue with the mist and two, would you be available for a conference call with everyone else later this afternoon. Tom and I feel that if we can all talk together, then we may be able to work through this."

"*Daniel* is on his way. I have *Mansfield* who can do *Daniel's* job just as well because I have trained all my team to be able to step into one another's job if needed, so you keep him until you are sure you no longer need him. Yes, I'll make sure that I'm available for the conference call later today.

Now both you boys take it *nice and slow* and don't rush into something you're not sure of. Read those books when you have time, especially your father's books and the last few of your grandfather's books.

I think that you might just be able to make *the greatest discovery* of the century and work out what will happen next and then you'll be able to put a stop to this mist once and for all." said Bennie.

Nikita turned to Tom and said "*Roy Rogers* is on the monitor and seems very disturbed. I think that you should talk to him next."

Tom turned to the monitor and said "Roy, what's up? You seem a little restless and upset?"

"*Earn while you learn Lord Choc Ice;* excuse me I have a communication to attend to." and then he turned his head and said "Tom, *if it wasn't for bad* reception that you guys had last night, I would have spoken to you then. I arrived here in *Sacrifice* only to find out that *Tiny Dancer* is nowhere to be found.

I sought out some of my *friends* who started asking their *friends* and eventually I found out that *Tiny Dancer* left *Sacrifice* with *Sweet Honesty* and they were heading for *Paris* so that Tiny could get some medical help.

The women never made it to Paris. Sweet Honesty was found asleep in one of the *Two Rooms at the End of the*

World Lodge in the town of *Soul Glove;* half way to Paris and Tiny again was nowhere to be found.

Reports state that she was last seen walking off with a blonde haired man with *blue eyes* and a nice smile.

All the girls love Alice because she knew the *ballad of a well-known gun* and was able to intercept some *madman across the water,* who was on his way over a walkway to cause some trouble with the blonde haired man and Tiny.

Even though *all the young girls love Alice* too, they all seemed to notice this strange blonde haired male and each gave a similar description of him to me, especially about his *blue eyes*.

What should I do now that Tiny is not here in *Sacrifice?"* said Roy.

"Roy. We have an unconfirmed report that *Tiny Dancer* is alright and she is with *Rocket Man* in *Crocodile Rock*.

Rocket Man is there on assignment, so *Tiny Dancer* would be able to help him. We haven't been able to talk to Tiny yet and find out how she managed to get from *Sacrifice* to *Crocodile Rock* and if that man who she was seen with really did help her in any way.

Would you please stay there in *Sacrifice* for the next week and report to us immediately if any strange events start happening, like a pale green mist covering the town or women walking in trance like states repeating "*Sorry seems to be the hardest word* to say but at least *I'm still standing* in *Philadelphia Freedom* because the *bitch is back*. *Sorry seems to be the hardest word* to say but at least *I'm still standing* in *Philadelphia Freedom* because the *bitch is back*." or something to that effect or if young boys and even girls start humming a tune and laughing uncontrollably.

If you do hear the children, please ask them what they are humming and if they tell you that *this song has no title;* get them to a medical centre, tell the authorities who you are and get them to give the children a sedative.

Sedated sleep seems to be the one thing that helps fight against the green mist also *I need you to turn to* your close friends only and ask for their help as well.

Will you be available to participate in a conference call this afternoon with our other people who are out in the field?" asked Tom.

"Yes. I'll make sure that I'm available for your conference and I will do everything I can while *I'm still standing* here to find out as much as I can about the man that Tiny went off with and the green mist." replied Roy.

Nikita turned to Harry and said "Tom is just finishing with *Roy Rogers* and I have satellite contact with Dan Dare and *Little Jeannie* in *Harmony* on monitor two. Go ahead Dan."

"Hi Harry." said Dan "I know that you wondering why both Little Jeannie and I are here together in Harmony. I will explain why I am here and then Jeannie can tell you her story.

I was just completing my training in the new craft in *Muse,* when a report was sent to my commander with orders for all available pilots and crews to man their ships and await further orders.

A military person approached my chief cabin crew member and I overheard him say "*Take me to the pilot* please and be prepared to take off as soon as you are given the clearance to do so.

Your pilot, co-pilot and navigator will be the only ones who will know your destination. During the flight your pilot will give you further instruction on what to do when you have reached your destination."

My orders were to fly to *Se Olvido* and collect some urgent and top secret supplies and deliver them to bases in *Sacrifice, Philadelphia Freedom, Your Song, Amoreena* on the *bad side of the moon,* Transvenus, Urallas and then on to *Harmony.*

My instructions were only to talk to the nominated personnel from each place about my mission and I only knew who to talk to once I had opened a sealed envelope after take-off from each place.

We had to be extra careful in *Sacrifice* and on Urallas.

We hadn't long left Urallas when one of my crew noticed a pale green mist floating towards Urallas. I looked at it and commented to the navigator that it was a strange sighting for this time of year. It is usually *in the summertime* that these weird sightings are recorded.

My navigator took some photos and noted the location of the mist on his charts for further reference.

It doesn't often snow at Christmas so *Philadelphia Freedom* is a *town of plenty* of ideas to *step into Christmas,* and *a change at Christmas......* can I put you on hold for a moment, I have just received an urgent communication from my commander.

Sorry, I have to go. I have been given some urgent orders and have to fly out immediately. I will now pass you over to *Little Jeannie.*

"Harry is Tom with you as I would like you both to hear this." said *Little Jeannie.* "As you know I was working undercover as the *part time love* of Cartier on Urallas.

One afternoon, about a week ago a person approached Cartier and offered to spend some time with him and that they had a deal for him that he couldn't refuse.

I am saying a person instead of a particular gender because although they looked like a *young, gifted and black* female, I am sure that that was just a disguise.

Cartier told them that the following *Saturday Night's alright* for their meeting about eight o'clock.

That Saturday I was fine, until about six o'clock in the evening and that's when I started to feel ill and by seven thirty I was being driven home by a blonde haired staff member of the *Scaffold* Underground Cavern who gave me some white powder to take.

I don't remember anything until I woke up well after eleven o'clock.

There seemed to be some panic happening on the street below and I heard someone shouting out "Cartier, *Did he shoot her?"* and the reply was

"Not the *young, gifted & black* female but he shot his other lovers, so his *loves lies bleeding* in different parts of town.

They say he has *one more arrow* and a *tinderbox* for his part time lover."

I knew that was me and I knew that I had to get out of town and quickly. I became scared when I heard a knock on my door, and then I recognized the voice of the man who had taken me home earlier that evening. I opened the door to see these two beautiful *blue eyes* looking at me with a sensuous smile just beneath them. I motioned for him to come in and I locked the door behind him.

I told him "I'm lucky *I'm still standing. Someone saved my life tonight* by making me ill and getting me out of the cavern.

You know there's *something about the way you look tonight* that is different from earlier today.

What happened when you got back to work?"

"My name is James and I have come back to make sure that you are alright. *I can't keep this from you;* someone shot Cartier and your *love lies bleeding* to death in the medical centre and everyone is saying that he would be *better off dead* because if he does pull through, his *end will come* when someone puts a *rope around a fool*'s neck.

He was warned that the female who had come to offer him the deal, was an *enchantment passing through* so *don't trust that woman* but his *ego* didn't want to listen.

He wanted to *wrap her up* in his *wicked dreams* and if it wasn't for the *Honky Tonk women* with their *Honky cat* who came in to listen to the blues, he would have gotten away with his plan. He even told them that *she sold me magic* so every *Honky cat* would be afraid of him.

Tonight has been the last straw for me. *It's hard to go back* and work in a place where there are continuing incidents and deaths happening. *I guess that's why they call it the blues* that you get while working in a place like that and I'm glad that *I'm still standing* and breathing after what has happened today.

You're not safe here anymore and it won't be long before your cover is blown; so *can I put you on* a shuttle tonight with the *Boogie Pilgrim,* who is a very close friend of mine. He will take you to stay in the *Tower Of Babel. Lady what's tomorrow?* ... Don't answer that; I remember.

My brain is a bit mixed up over today's proceedings. I have to stay here until tomorrow afternoon but I will meet up with you in the early evening of tomorrow.

Boogie has a saying which is "*Don't let the sun go down on me* until I'm all *signed sealed and delivered* to our maker." and I feel the same."

I was just about to ask him how he knew that I was undercover when the sound of thunder in the night was heard that sent the people in the streets screaming and scattering for shelter.

James looked like he was listening to something or someone and then he turned and grabbed my purse and two *leather jackets* from the back of a chair, threw one jacket at me whist saying "put this on." and then ushered me out my door and down the stairs.

He said "That is not ordinary thunder; it is a sign that there is more trouble on the way and I need to get you out of here before it comes and spreads *heartache all over the world*.

I can't allow you to stay here and *sweat it* out and it's going to be very risky taking you outside. There is something *in the air tonight* that is dangerous for you to breathe. *I stop and I breathe* in the air and it doesn't affect me but it will affect you badly."

Then I heard in the distance many women's voices saying repeatedly "*Sorry seems to be the hardest word* to say in *Philadelphia Freedom* and *don't let the sun go down on me* because the *bitch is back. Sorry seems to be the hardest word* to say in *Philadelphia Freedom* and *don't let the sun go down on me* because the *bitch is back*."

We both then heard "*Ho, Ho, Ho...Ho, Ho, Ho, Who'd be a turkey at Christmas* because *I don't wanna go on with you like that.*"

A man yelled out "Quick *cage the songbird* before it starts singing his *last song* and becomes a *high flying bird* that we won't be able to catch. *I need you to turn to* the bird and give it all your attention in an effort to keep it calm."

James said as he was pulling down the *curtains* "Too late. Here take this white powder now. It won't hurt you; I promise."

I didn't ask any questions but I took the powder that had a fizzy orange taste and I don't remember anything else until I woke up about two hours later as one of the *passengers* on Dan Dare's craft.

It seemed quite unusual to see that most of his passengers were women who were either still asleep or just waking up.

A few of Dan's crew attended to the women and separated the ones who were waking up confused from the still sleeping ones

I must have some sort of amnesia because I can't remember what happened or where we were taken to after that.

Tom said "I'm glad that you are safe now and alright. What you have just told us has been very interesting. Will you be available to join in a conference call later this afternoon with a few other people from our agency?

I will have to wait until Dan can continue talking to us so that we can find out how you got on his craft and where he took you and the rest of the women."

"Yes, I'll be here and I will do what I can to help you because of what I have seen and heard lately. There is a lot more trouble looming and we need to find a way to stop it.

Last night I thought "*Someone saved my life tonight.*" and today I'm glad that *I'm still standing* as a normal female." replied *Little Jeannie.*

MAPS, CHARTS AND MARKERS

Carla Etude was the next person that they spoke to and she was still in *Cottonfields;* however, she was just about to book out of the *Cottonfields Country Comfort* Motel and head back home to *Your Song.*

"Carla." said Harry "I know that this can be inconvenient for you but would you be able to stay down there for a few more days please.

Teacher I need you to find out as much as you can of the past history and unusual events that have happened in *Cottonfields.* I know that the *Country Comfort* Motel is one of the oldest buildings there.

I also need you to find out as much as you can about a place called *Goodbye Yellow Brick Road* Mansion.

At the moment, we are aware that there is a pale green mist covering the universe and it can have different effects on different people. We would like to know if *Cottonfields* have had this mist in the area recently. If they haven't and it comes; don't go outside or get anywhere near it as it can be very dangerous; especially for women.

I would like you to join in our conference later today so that you can hear more about what is happening from our other people in the field. Would you be available?"

"Yes. I will be available. If this mist is covering the universe, would you be able to find out if my mother and sisters on *Your Song* are safe and unaffected please. They live in a little town called *Mellow* which is a few miles north and *up around the bend* of the *Sails* River?" replied Carla.

"I'll get a message through to *Bennie and the Jets* who are on *Your Song* right now, and I'll get them to tell you how your family is during the conference call." said Tom.

"Captain Fantastic and the Brown Dirt Cowboys are on monitor three." said

Nikita and then she added *"Daniel* was right, he told me that if I set my monitors and sets to five, five one we would get better communication links with everyone, including Captain Fantastic and the Brown Dirt Cowboys, even if they are on the *bad side of the moon."*

"Tom. I was a bit worried about you because you never returned our communication last night.

There is a pale green mist causing havoc out there in *Levon* and now it has started causing havoc in *Amoreena* on the *bad side of the moon.*

I have left *Gulliver* and half of the Cowboys in *Levon* and the rest of us should be touching down in *Amoreena* in about five minutes. *Can I put you on* hold till we land or would you like me to call you back?" said Captain Fantastic.

Harry answered "Instead of calling us back, would you be available to sit in on a conference call late this afternoon, or I should say for you this morning. This will give you a chance to find out what is going on out there."

"That's a great idea." said Captain Fantastic. "I'll get *Grimsby* to contact *Levon* and if it's alright with you, could we also include them in the conference. Everybody will know what's going on then and will be able to have an input, and then I won't have to remember and repeat what has been discussed."

After having a short break from the communications, for a cup of coffee, Nikita and the boys tried several times to get a connection with *Rocket Man* or *Tiny Dancer*. *Rocket Man* was the one who finally answered.

"*Rocket Man* is *Tiny Dancer* with you and how is she?" asked Harry.

Rocket Man replied in a very quiet voice "Yes, she is here with me but she is just waking up. She seems to sleep a lot; more than what you would expect from a person like her.

Unfortunately I haven't been able to find out much on the *madman across the water* except that he often goes to *Your Song* for a few days each fortnight.

He is a regular *Saturday night* traveller

on the direct *Skyline Pigeon* flight to *Your Song* and he travels back here to *Crocodile Rock* on a *Wednesday night* via the *Skyline Pigeon* Intercapital shuttle and the *Crazy Water* River Night Cruises.

I've heard that *Saturday night's alright* when flying the direct *Sky line Pigeon* flight to *Your Song* because they have live entertainment on board, called *Duets for One*.

When I bought Tiny back here, we travelled on the train, thinking that it would pull in here but when it didn't, I asked the guard why and he told me "*This train don't stop there anymore.*"

We had to get off at *Brokeback Mountain* and I knew that once again I would have to say another *goodbye Yellow Brick Road;* believe me it is the worst road in the universe to travel on.

I was visiting a very *old friend* of mine in *Sacrifice* and I heard about the green mist but I didn't think anything about it until some of the females there went into a trance like state and started saying repeatedly "*Sorry seems to be the hardest word* to say, so *don't let the sun go down on me* in *Philadelphia Freedom* because the *bitch is back*. *Sorry seems to be the hardest word* to say, so *don't let the sun go down on me* in *Philadelphia Freedom* because the *bitch is back*."

My friend and I wandered through the streets looking at the unbelievable sight of all these women in a trance like state; but not only that, there were young children having bouts of uncontrollable laughter between humming an unusual tune. I even asked one of the children what the name of the tune was and they told me that "*this song has no title*."

It was then that I saw *Tiny Dancer* being ushered down an alley way. Who in this universe could not miss noticing Tiny with her blue hair, so I followed them?

Tiny was put in the back of a van and then another female wearing an unusual lower face mask got in the back with Tiny and drove to the end of the alley and turned left into *Grey Seal* Street.

I knew that the street was only a one way street that led to the main road out of town. I asked my friend to make some urgent enquiries and find out who the people were and where they might have taken Tiny.

A report from some *talking old soldiers* was that the other female was Sweet Honesty and they heading to somewhere past Soul Glove.

It was the following day, when I was leaving my friend's place to come here to *Crocodile Rock* that Tiny turned up at my friend's front door with a *meal ticket* in her hand.

I couldn't help but notice this tall guy with blonde hair and *blue eyes* standing across the street watching Tiny but with the blink of an eye he disappeared when he saw me standing in the doorway.

Tiny didn't look too bad but her speech was a bit sloppy and she asked if she could come to *Crocidile Rock* with me because as she said and I quote "*I'm still standing* because *someone saved my life tonight* and told me that I'm not safe here on my own anymore." I bought her back here and that is what I was trying to report to you yesterday but your communication systems were not working and that in its self, seemed very odd.

Only once before has your communication systems not work at all and that was *sixty* years ago. I remember granddad telling me that he was on his way back from *Border Song* by the Intercity shuttle when something happened and he tried to get in touch with your father but couldn't get through.

He had to ask one of the crew to *take me to the pilot* who then made a slight detour and set him down near Brokeback Mountain to catch the train home.

Dad asked the train driver before he got on if the train stopped at Crocodile Rock and the driver said "*This train don't stop there anymore.*" so he knew that once again that he would have to say another *goodbye Yellow Brick Road*.

He told me that the communications were fine the following day."

Rocket Man turned to Tiny and said "Harry and Tom want to talk to you. Are you up to talking to them now?"

Harry asked *Rocket Man* if he would sit in on the conference that he was organizing for later that day and was told that he would.

Tiny Dancer's face appeared on the monitor and it was Tom who spoke to her first "Hi Tiny, how are you feeling? Are you up to answering some questions for us please?"

Tiny replied "After saying *goodbye Yellow Brick Road,* I guess I'm alright and I'll answer questions for you just as long as my memory will work. At the moment *I can't tell the bottom from the top* or is it *I can't tell the top from the bottom.*"

Harry stopped Tom from asking the questions and instead said "Tiny, we know that you have been through a lot over the past few days so why don't you tell us what you can remember. We'll work it out from there but I must ask you first, did a tall blonde man help you at all?"

With the mention of the blonde male, Tiny seemed to brighten up and she started talking. "*Can you feel the love tonight?* You know love is just like a *candle in the wind* and if you are not careful and tend to it, it can just go out suddenly. *My baby left me one day* for a *Natural Sinner* from the outer galaxy of *Tierra* where *there's no tomorrow* only the *original sin* whatever it is.

He will be happy with the *Natural Sinner* because *my baby loves lovin'* all the time and now he can even have it *all across the Havens* as well, can't he?"

Tina shook her head then continued "I was on my way to *Entre Paredes* to check out something about a plan to murder a king and to visit *Lucy in the sky with diamonds* and warn her of a plan to steal some of her diamonds.

It was when I was looking out the craft's window and I saw *three little birds* disappear into a pale green cloud and I knew that something was wrong. I said to one of the cabin crew "*Take me to the pilot;* it's a matter of urgency."

I spoke to the pilot and he changed his course for *Sacrifice.*

One of the female crew went into a

trance like state and started saying something like "*Sorry seems to be the hardest word* to say and *I don't want to go on with you like that* because *the b**** is back. Sorry seems to be the hardest word* to say and *I don't want to go on with you like that* because *the b**** is back.*"

I think that a few more women did the same thing."

Tiny's face seemed to go trance like when she said "When *the day is done* and the *sunshine of your love* has gone, there is only one place left to go; that is to the *club at the end of the street* and listen to the *blues*. The blues are not always *sad songs* but the *blues never fade away*. Even the *blues for my baby and me* that the *piano man, Big Dipper* used to play for us, will sound just as good without him; he can have his *Natural Sinner*.

Really *nobody wins* when they play the game of love and all they can say to each other is "*Don't go breaking my heart.*" which is eventually broken."

Rocket Man gave Tiny a drink of cloudy water and then she said "The blonde haired man who had *blue eyes* also seemed to show security through his smile and he did help me.

I felt very safe with him and he looked like *Daniel,* one of *Bennie and the Jets*. I knew that *someone saved my life tonight* and I was *blessed* that he came along when he did because I could see the *teardrops* in people's eyes as they realized that their *hearts have turned to stone*.

I think the green mist could bring *heartache all over the world* and the universe if an antidote is not found for it. Please *don't let the sun go down on me,* get me under cover until this universe becomes safe again.

I don't remember much more at this present moment but give me a day or two to refresh my memory and myself and get some more of my strength back.

I do know that the blonde hair man told me more than I remember so I hope that returns soon as well.

I heard you ask Rocket Man to join in a conference later today; well, may I join in too. Something may be said that could jog my memory?"

"You certainly may join in but only if you are feeling up to it. I don't want you to tire yourself out too much." replied Tom.

Nikita left the room while Tiny was talking and when she walked back in she said "*Come and get it.*" and the boys turned to see her heading to the main table carrying a tray with three plates on it; one of mixed savory crackers, another with the last of the Honey Roll and Lemon *Bitter Fingers* and on the third were the last two *Jack Rabbit* pies that had been heated.

There was also a pot of freshly brewed coffee balancing itself between the plates.

Tom looked at the savory crackers and commented that they didn't look like the meat from his tins.

Nikita replied "I have tried your brand of tin food and I didn't like it very much so I went *back to Paramount.* I personally think that Paramount tastes a lot nicer and fresher than your brand of Aquarium John does.

It has been a long and interesting morning so I thought that before you boys sit down and work through what you have already found out, a nourishing break would be in order. The break will also refresh your minds as well."

"*Thank you mama.*" said Tom jokingly. "I know that I could do with a cup of that coffee right now."

"Nikita, are there many detailed maps or charts of the universe in the office; especially ones that cover the areas where our people who are out in the field are?" asked Tom questioningly.

"Why yes, I think there are. I am pretty sure that there are maps and charts of some sort down in my room. Shall I'll go and get them? asked Nikita.

"Yes please. I have had a thought that I will explain to both of you once I have had a look of the maps and charts." replied Tom.

Nikita was gone for almost ten minutes before returning with an armful of rolled maps and charts balancing on top of two very large books that she dropped down on the big conference table. "This is all I could find." she said. "What do you want them for?"

"Yes Tom." said Harry "What do you want them for? Please explain yourself."

Tom didn't say anything but laid all the maps out on one section of the table and then he laid the charts out on another section.

He walked back and forth between the two lots and swapped different section of the maps around until he was happy with their lay out and then he did the same with the charts.

A couple of pieces of the maps had a green marking on them and so did the corresponding charts. He stood there looking at and analyzing both the maps and charts for five minute, making notes every now and then.

"Just as I thought." said Tom.

"Just as you thought what." said Harry

walking over to him.

Tom pointed to the maps and said "These are all the places in the universe and these are the places where our field agents are at the moment." As Tom pointed them out he place a small marker on each spot.

He continued saying "Right now; we are here on the Moon and Carla Etude is in *Cottonfields,* down on Earth.

Benny and the Jets are on *Your Song* and Dan Dare was on the Little *Your Song*ulis Military Base. Captain Fantastic and the Brown Dirt Cowboys are now in two smaller groups; one group here in *Levon* on Urallas and the other group is now in *Amoreena* on the *bad side of the moon.*

Tiny Dancer was on her way to Entregate to see *Lucy in the sky with diamonds* but ended up in *Sacrifice,* note both places are on Transvenus and Roy Rogers is still in *Sacrifice. Little Jeannie* was also on Urallas but *in Neon.*

Both Dan and *Little Jeannie* got together in *Harmony* on The *Crystal*

Planet and *Rocket Man* was sent to *Crocodile Rock* on the distant planet of Hot *Encore.*

Look at the pattern where all our people are on the maps. Now look at the charts and tell me what do you see?"

"What, *I can't tell the bottom from the top."* and Harry looked again and amazingly said "All those markers make an ancient destructive sign, don't they?"

Harry walked around the table looking at the map and then said "Wait a minute, Nikita come here for a minute please.

Last night when you thought I spoke to you, what places did you say that you were supposed to be visiting? I'm sure that you will remember and as you say the places, I want to put a different color marker on them."

"I thought that you told me that out of the blue on the day after New Year's Day, I will have to attend a meeting at the *Seasons Reprise* Conference Centre on *Your Song* with *Lady D'Arbanville, Lady Samantha* and the *Island girl,* then I will have to go to *Border Song* on Mandalay and meet a man who will give me a letter.

I will then have to deliver the letter to the man with all the toys on Earth. I will then visit our *friends, Rocket Man* and *Tiny Dancer* in *Levon* and not to forget that I *gotta get a meal ticket* each time I want to eat out.

Rocket Man will then take me to St Peter who will then escort me to *Val-Hala* where I will find warm love in a cold world.

Then you said something about *you can make history,* religion rehearsals, *recover your soul* and *written in the stars* that I didn't hear properly and I wanted you to repeat." said Nikita.

Harry finished putting the different color markers on the places that Nikita mentioned, pausing for a few moments before placing the last marked on Nubia.

Sheepishly Harry said "I forgot for a moment where Val-Hala was. Now look at the map and tell me now what you see."

Surprisingly Tom said "Those markers have just changed the ancient destructive sign to a winners *power* sign; Today's sign of recognition that all our winners receive no matter how big or small the win is.

Now look at the green marks on the maps and charts and what do they show you?"

"They also mark out a *circle of life* around the power sign; see this marker and those two markers are the ones that make the full circle." and using her finger to point she continued saying "That's where the green mist has been reported so far.

There are a few places that have not reported seeing it yet and one of them is the planet of Nubia.

If these charts are right, shouldn't we try to warn them of the mist and that it may be heading their way." said Nikita.

Tom thought for a moment and then asked Harry "What do you think that dad would do. I am not sure if I would want to let this green mist's destinations become common knowledge especially as we are not certain whether we have made the right assumption.

I wish that dad was here or even *Daniel* because I feel that he would know if we are on the right track or not.

How long will it take for him to get back here?"

"Not as long as you think." replied *Daniel* as he walked through the Boardroom door "I thought that all of you would be up here as it is the best place for you all to be.

As soon as you requested my assistance, Bennie told me to get the fastest transport back here.

I had Dan Dare come and pick me up as he was at the Little *Your Song*ulis Military Base and that's not that far away from *Your Song*. Dan knew the urgency of my getting here so he flew faster than a *high flying bird* with a tail wind.

Now, what is it that you want me to help you out with?"

Tom and Harry showed Daniel the maps and charts on the table and explained about the markers.

They also showed him the difference

between the signs that the markers made and the circle of life.

Tom pointed out where the green mist had already been and by the charts, where the mist was going. It seemed that it was going to be *all quiet on the western front* because it had already passed over that section.

Then he said "We were debating as to whether or not we should warn the planets of the possibility of it coming to them and also suggesting methods for preparing for it. We think that Nubia is next in line for the green mist. Should we warn them?"

"Nubia is already prepared for its arrival. A *spirit in the sky* has warned them and they have all the children and women inside a specially built and safe place.

The men, so far, have never been affected and *sixty years on* from the last time it came, we are hoping that it still doesn't affect them." said *Daniel*.

"Now, I think that it's time for us to prepare for the conference call this afternoon. We have to work out what we know about this pale green mist, so that if there are many differences from what our people in the field tells us, then we can inform them of our discoveries.

Daniel, after you have read our findings; would you please tell us if you have any more to add to it?" said Tom.

Harry handed *Daniel* all the information that they had gathered about the pale green mist, including the books that made reference to it and asked him to read it. Nikita gave *Daniel* a cup of coffee and cleared the smaller table for him to work on.

Nikita went up to Tom and Harry and asked "Yesterday, after *Rocket Man* had arrived and was sitting in your office, Tom and I came in and informed you about *Tiny Dancer* being found in *Sacrifice* and how Tom had sent Roy Rogers to get her. Do you both remember that?

I was wondering why *Rocket Man* got so upset about you not sending him and why he went to visit an old friend in

Sacrifice first instead of heading to *Crocodile Rock* to commence the assignment that you had just given him.

I also can't understand why he took Tiny to *Crocodile Rock* with him instead of bringing or sending her here for medical treatment. I feel that there is something going on with *Rocket Man* that we don't know of."

Tom replied to Nikita "I have been reading in those books from my grandfather's era that he felt that there was a strong connection between the *madman across the water* and *Rocket Man*.

There was also a couple of pages on how the *Flintstone boy* used to live on *Christmas Island* on Earth and one day his wife, who had become very ill, told him just before she died "*Don't let the sun go down on me,* take me to *Sick City* if you have to. You have to kill *all the nasties* of this Bacterial *Social Disease* if you want to stop it spreading. Keep *Amy* away from me because *to be young, gifted and black* like she is...."

They state that this was the beginning of his depression and the *first episode at Hienton* was a month after saying *goodbye* to his wife when he said *goodbye England's Rose* at a *funeral for a friend* and two weeks after that, he said *Goodbye Marlon Brando* at another *funeral for a friend.*

Marlon had died from the same bacterial disease that his wife had had. It also states that he went back to where he was living and knocked holes all around the base and walls of his house in anger.

He slammed the front door one day as he was leaving with his daughter *and the house fell down,* so he took a craft to *Your Song* and tried to settle there with his cousin *Pied Pauper* and his wife *Angeline.*

He must have been *born to lose* because it states that he lost *Amy* to the same Bacterial *Social Disease* that had also killed his wife.

He then moved to *Crocodile Rock* and became known as the *madman across the water.* He still visited his cousin on *Your Song* quite often and one day he came home with a very young boy named Guy and some strange packages and plants.

His father made up a *song for Guy* and sang it to him frequently and one day his cousin Pied, who was visiting, asked him about it and was told that it was just a *song for Guy.*

During that visit, Guy became ill with all the symptoms of Bacterial *Social Disease* and the madman became very hysterical over the thought of losing his son but Pied gave Guy some sort of liquid to drink that eventually saved him.

Nobody who lived across the river ever saw or heard about the boy again, even though they knew that he was alive and they often heard the sound of the *song for Guy* floating across the water."

Daniel interrupted them by saying "I think that we should get ready for the conference now.

I feel that you should listen to what the others have to say but mention little of what you have found out. You can always have another conference tomorrow after you have sorted through all the information given to you.

I will set up the old text type recorder and printer so that we can record and print out what has been said by each person and no one will know because today's technology will not pick it up."

Nikita looked puzzled and said "I think that the story of *Rocket Man* is quite confusing because I have just read something else that is quite different to what you had to say unless there are two people who wear the same outfit and goes under the name of *Rocket Man*. I must admit that when *Rocket Man* comes in here, he never takes off his helmet so I never see his face.

Have you seen his face at all?"

CONFERENCE CALL

Nikita and *Daniel* set the monitors, type text recorder and printer on the main conference table along with note pads and pens, and he told her "*Your starter for it* all will be when you turn the sets on."

The maps and charts were moved down towards one end of the table so that they could be referred to quite easily. *Daniel* operated the main communication controls and monitors and as he contacted each person who was going to be involved in the conference, he asked them "*Can I put you on* hold while I join you all together?"

The third party he contacted was Roy Rogers who asked "Daniel, would it be possible for me to talk with Harry in private before the conference begins. I have some very important information that I feel that he would like to know about before the meeting?"

Daniel diverted Roy to Harry's personal computer where they were able to have a short confidential meeting.

Harry was heard to say "Well, when *talking old soldiers* like to talk, they really do have something to say.

It sounds like we may have a *ticking* time bomb out there. No, at the present moment I don't need to carry *my father's gun* but I will keep it close at hand in the future. If he wants it then he'll have to *come and get it."*

Then Harry called out "We've finished here so *whenever you're ready,* we can begin the conference."

Bennie was the first to speak "You boys really have jumped *into the old man's shoes* and you are both handling this issue very well. Harry or Tom, I do need to speak with either of you privately after this conference is over if either of you are available?

The *Island girl* was not Emily but her sister Alice and she was not able to give us much information except she remembers that she was *chasing the crown* on the clown's head with the younger children at the *Whitewash*

County Amusement park when a man dressed like *Hercules* called to her. It was the first time that *Hercules* had ever come to *Your Song*.

She went over to him and he said to her "*My baby left me* for the *Mona Lisas and Mad Hatters* in *Philadelphia Freedom* so I get *no valentines* anymore." and as he gave her a *black icy stare,* she felt a sudden puff of wind on her face; like a *candle in the wind* being blown out and she doesn't remember anything after that. Whatever her parents gave her must have been strong because she has just woken up.

It seems that *all the girls love Alice* and she was with the children three days ago. I've contacted each family and all the other children are fine.

I did notice that there was a very light bruise on the *Island girl*'s hand where someone might have been trying to remove some blood from her or inject her with something.

I would like to bring her back in the next day or two so that our medical team can make sure that she has not been injected with a virus or something to that nature."

Rocket Man looked nervous as he interrupted quickly and commented "If she was running around with other children, then she might have run into something and hit herself.

Why do you have to think that someone was trying to do harm to her. You are *never too old* to hurt yourself by running into objects."

"Yes, I suppose you're right, she could have done it herself but the *Holy Mother* of the *Sisters of the Cross,* who attends to their church, has known the *Island girl* since she has been born and feels that the girl is still unwell.

A check up for her will not do any harm and it will put a few people's minds to rest knowing that she is alright.

Carla your mother and sister are fine and they send you their best wishes." replied Bennie.

Tom noticed that when *Rocket Man* was on the monitor, in the background he could see Tiny standing against the wall but she seemed very unsteady on her feet and in her hand was a glass of cloudy water and he thought "I wonder what she is drinking? It is not like Tiny to drink anything but clear liquids even if she was in severe *pain* or had a headache."

The conference was going fairly well. *Gulliver* and the Brown Dirt Cowboys had settled the matter in *Levon* and were preparing to leave for the *bad side of the moon* the following morning.

Harry asked Captain Fantastic if he would mind leaving them there for another couple of days if he didn't really need them.

Dan Dare was still on his mission so he couldn't partake in the conference but when *Little Jeannie* came on screen, she saw Daniel and surprisingly said "James, what are you doing there. I thought that you would be at the *Tower of Babel* with your *friends?*

Are you working there now?"

Daniel replied "I'm sorry, but I am not

James. I'm Daniel, one of *Bennie and the Jets* boys and I am just here to help Harry and Tom out for a short while."

"Oh!" said *Little Jeannie* surprised "but you look just like the man who helped me get off Urallas. I am very thankful to him because *I'm still standing* and I'm very much alive.

Tom, Harry, I don't really remember much more than what I told you earlier today.

For some reason though, five names come to mind but I only know one of them. Could you put *Rocket Man* on screen as I think he might know of four of them?"

It was a matter of seconds before Little Jeannie was having face to face contact with *Rocket Man* and she asked him "Do you recall having any contact with three men named *Pinball Wizard, Razor Face* and *Stinker on Dark Street* in *Sacrifice*.

I don't think that you would know of *Beates Medley* because I met him later in *Allentown* on the *Slow Rivers* ferry that looks *just like Noah's Ark*.

He gave me a letter to pass on to *Ying Yang Tu,* who is with St Peter at the moment, conveying this message "The letter has been passed on through *Japanese hands* and now it is *signed, sealed, delivered* to the right person." and now Mr. *Medley* could go to the *Original Sin* Blues Club to listen to some *sad songs. I guess that's why they call it the blues* because the *sad songs* can bring you down and make you feel *sad* or the *sad songs say so much* to someone and that it makes them happy."

Tom watched *Rocket Man* very closely while Little Jeannie was talking to him. The first four men that he was asked about, Rocket Man tried to act as calmly as possible and denied knowing them but when Japanese Hands and the *Original Sin* Blues Club was mentioned, he became a bit more agitated than what he was.

To make it look like it was not what Little Jeannie had asked him, he turned his head away and called out "Hey, you guys turn that music down.

You know that *sad songs* agitate me and I'm on a conference call here."

Tom said "Seeing that we are with you, will you get Tiny to the monitor so that we can talk to her?"

"Hi Tom, I'm sorry that I had to say *goodbye Yellow Brick Road.*" said Tiny "*Can you feel the love tonight;* it's floating around you or maybe there's *something about the way you look tonight* that makes me want to ask you "*are you ready for love* and if you are, then *come and get it.*

Don't go breaking my heart by not coming. If love is like a *candle in the wind* and it doesn't go out, then, used unwisely it could *burn down the mission* and leave a lot of *burning buildings.*"

Before she could say anymore Daniel looked into her eyes through the monitor and said very quietly, "Tiny, *someone saved my life tonight* and *I'm still standing* because of him. *We all fall in loves sometimes* but if the *candle in the wind* goes out we have to ask "*Where to now St Peter?* and he will tell us."

Tiny spat out the mouthful of drink and shook her head before saying "Please *don't let the sun go down on me* here anymore. *Crocodile Rock* is *too low for zero* during the day and it is even colder at night. There's a place not far from here called *Jingle Bell Rock* and it's *just like Belgium* and is much warmer than here and I want to move there.

Who would think that on a planet called Hot *Encore,* there would be a place called *Crocodile Rock* that is *too low for zero.*"

A hand was seen giving Tiny a glass of cloudy water but as she tried to brush it away their monitor went dead.

Nikita, who had been watching Tiny, said "We have to find a way to get her back here as soon as possible. She has gotten worse since she last spoke to us. Each time we see her, she has a drink of cloudy liquid in her hand but what is it that she is drinking or been given to drink?"

Bennie, who had also been watching the whole proceedings, stated "*Daniel,* you help the boys to get Tiny back before more unpleasant things happen to her. I think that you know that she is in grave danger and needs our help.

Carla you have been watching too, so *teacher I need you* to find a *travelin' band* that can get you to *Crocodile Rock* in a hurry and I'll arrange for you to meet and stay with *Layla*.

With her help you might be able to find out what is in the water there that makes it cloudy.

The rest of us had better make our way back to the Moon because when *Rocket Man* finds out about what is going on, he will come after Tom, Harry and certainly Nikita."

Captain Fantastic said "You boys in *Levon* leave there tonight and pick up Little Jeannie and bring her to the Moon and once you have her safely with Tom and Harry, then come round and join us on the *bad side of the moon*.

Roy, I have heard comments of "*There goes a well known gun.*" once you have walked past people, may I suggest that you leave *Sacrifice* as soon as you can and join me on the bad side of the Moon. United we stand and will be stronger to take on Rocket Man.

With *Bennie and the Jets* coming in from one way and the rest of us coming in from the opposite direction, I am hoping that Rocket Man won't want to fight but if he does then I think that *Saturday night's alright for fighting* with us."

Roy commented "I can't believe that the *first episode at Hienton* all those years ago could have turned Rocket Man into the person he has become.

As long as *I'm still standing* I will not let anyone destroy the agency that Mr. Brumby has built to protect the citizens of this universe.

I feel like a bullet or two may not even be enough to stop him. I don't even think that *Hercules* could get near him and *Hercules* is a mighty big and strong man.

I won't come back in Old 67 because she's too slow but I will take an express *Skyline Pigeon* flight and ask one of the cabin crew to *take me to the pilot.*

I'll show him my credentials and ask him to take me to the *Vive Retreat* as I have to *get back* urgently to attend and be security at a *funeral for a friend* who is a high profile dignitary.

Once I *get back,* I'll send you the coded signal that will say "*Goodbye Yellow Brick Road"* and you can send *your son* to pick me up from the *empty garden* at the old abandoned *Holiday Inn.*"

"*Goodbye Yellow Brick Road.*" said Captain Fantastic "I haven't used that code for nearly two decades. Mr. Brumby made it up when he was a bit younger than his boys are now. I can't remember how it came about now. Do you still remember Roy?"

"Yes, I was with him." said Roy "Now you boys listen as I suspect that this will be something that you wouldn't have heard of before.

Mr. Brumby and I were on our way back to *Sin Ti* after a meeting with *Bennie & the Jets* at the *Grey Seal* Naval Base when we saw two *freaks in love* heading our way.

We heard one of them saying "Don't give him the *hard luck story,* just say *can you feel the love tonight* and if you can, *are you ready for love* because *I want love* and let's *give peace a chance* before the *candle in the wind* is blown out and while you're keeping him busy; I'll hood wink him for his money pouch."

They hadn't seen me behind your father and your father thought that there might be trouble so he told me to go and stand behind the tree to our left.

He said that if there was any trouble he would not *yell help* but say *goodbye Yellow Brick Road.* That would be the signal for me to show myself with my gun ready to fire whilst whistling the *Ballad of a Well known Gun.*

Your father said "*I feel like a bullet* fired in the air would stop anything from happening." and they would continue walking down the *cold highway.*

Well, your father was right and we used that code many times after that and we taught it to our field officers in case they ever needed a backup call for help.

Now, I have said enough so *whenever you're ready* to get started, I'm ready."

Bennie looked through the monitor at the boys and replied "Oh, *take me back* to those good old days. I remember that the *Ballad of a Well-known Gun, Michelle's song* and the *Texan Love song* were the most popular songs of the time. I heard the other day a *variation on Michelle's song* but it wasn't as good as the original.

It seems that although the *Pinball Wizard* and *all the nasties* from our days are either locked up for good or dead; there always seems to be another one to take their place. I can't *believe* that Rocket Man has turned out to be a serious threat to us seeing that he was one of our field officers.

I am with Roy when I say that *I feel like a bullet* is not going to stop him and what's more worrying is that he has *Tiny Dancer* with him who he can use as a hostage.

He is keeping her in a kind of trance so that she can't defend herself.

Right now the Jets are preparing to leave *Your Song* and we should be back there tomorrow morning at the latest.

Daniel, you help out as much as you can and ask *dear God* to send you some more of your brilliant ideas. They always seem to work without much fuss or blood shed. *Goodbye* from me."

GREAT DISCOVERIES OR NOT

Tom said "I think that I have just made *the greatest discovery* that will solve a part of this dilemma. I honestly *believe* that the bitch is not a female as we are led to *believe* but a male. I'm not quite sure yet but we may even know who he is. This book that dad wrote has a few more chapters that I want to read before I can consolidate his findings.

He seemed so close to solving the mystery of the pale green mist and I wonder why he never did solve it before he retired?"

"Phew. I thought that we might have both made the same *greatest discovery* but I think that I have figured out what creates the pale green mist and how it is keeps going and multiplies. There is one thing I do know and that is; the mist that is affecting the people of today is not its natural source but one that has been manipulated over many years.

You were right when you stated that dad was close to solving the mist mystery. When he comes in later this week, we should ask him why he was unable to finally solve the mystery." commented Harry.

Tom put down the book and muttered "Rocket Man, the bitch is Rocket Man. I know that he may not be of the human life form but I am not aware of any other life form that eventually does not die.

These books go back nearly three hundred years and the Rocket Man has been mention right from the beginning. Even great, great grandfather mentions that he was with the agency before he took over and eventually bought it out."

"*You may be right,* you know. *It's me that you need* to put all your theories and conclusions together." said his father standing listening at the door of the Boardroom. "I came back as soon as I found out that the mist had reappeared again.

It has been nearly *sixty years on* from the last outbreak in my adolescent years and that was nearly *sixty years on* from the outbreak in my father's time. Each time the mist appears there is a *variation on* who it controls and how it controls them and where it travels to."

"Dad." shouted Tom "we weren't expecting you for another couple of days. We didn't expect that you would come back into the office so soon seeing that you have just retired."

"Dad, are we glad that you're here. We certainly can use your help in trying to solve the issue of the pale green mist. Tom, Nikita and I, have been reading through these books and each of us finds something interesting in them and once we have spoken to the others about it, it seems to coincide with what one us have read in the books that we were reading." said Harry.

"Nikita, would you please get me a cup of coffee and then turn the communications to night mode before you come and join us. I have some explaining to do." asked Mr. Brumby.

It took Nikita a few minutes to do as she was asked.

"Right now; where do I begin?" said Mr. Brumby. "I suppose I should start with the books and work backwards.

There is a reason why I never told you boys about the books and that is; I have not retired as everyone thinks but I have been out investigating and verifying the results of my many years of work. I have the last two copies of my books right here in my jacket pocket.

I did go to the *Holiday Inn* on *Your Song* as I told you; but I also arranged to meet with St Peter there?

He has been helping me with my research since I was a boy and we have made many great discoveries but the *greatest discovery* of all was how the pale green mist was made and what it is made from in its original form.

Feliz Navidad was my best friend and was also helping me with my research and I found out two hours after he had *gone to Shiloh* on business for me that for some reason, that I won't mention just yet, his train became a *runaway train* that derailed on *the bridge* that was *up around the bend* from his destination.

A part of the train fell into the *Screw You* River but Feliz had disappeared. There were only two people on that *runaway train* that were not counted for or found; one was the train driver and the other was Feliz and still today nobody knows if they are dead or alive. I do *believe* that Feliz is dead but the train driver is still alive.

Billy Bones and the white bird that he travels with survived and stated that the driver left the cabin in a hurry and quickly walked back through the train just before the derailment.

He also stated that he stopped the driver and asked if the train stopped at the *Tight Rope* Station and the driver replied that *this train don't stop there anymore* and hurried on.

A couple of other passengers who survived remembered *Billy Bones and the white bird* and verified his story.

To get to the *big picture* as I am seeing

it now, you have to *come down in time* and work backwards and not forwards.

The technology of today is so advanced from my father's era and his father's era that looking at the issue from their perspective is so much more time consuming. If you take what has been put down in *writing* and analyze it, you will get very confused.

St Peter has been entering all the information from these books and a few other manuscripts onto a computer analyzing disc and has come to a couple of very interesting conclusions.

I had to ask *"Where to now St. Peter?"* and before he had a chance to give me a solid reply, the green mist started to appear again and he was called away to help the *Princess of Gray Seal* get back to her home in *Georgia*.

I left the *Holiday Inn* on *Your Song* just after St. Peter and was standing at the *crossroads* when I heard a few voices talking about when they tried to *burn down the mission* not far from there because the Holy Mother looked down on them and their *three way love affair.* Because of the *heavy traffic,* it took about five minutes before we could all cross the road, but before we did cross I heard a strange version of the *song for Guy* coming from an apartment window just behind me. My father had a very faint recording of it given to him by someone who knew the *madman across the water* in *Crocodile Rock.*

I walked down *Blue Avenue* towards the *Celos* Diner and three *Honky Tonk women,* all carrying a *Honky cat,* approached me and asked if I knew how they could get to the *Screw You* River Blues Club.

One of the women said that DBR played the most exquisite blues music and *sad songs* that she had ever heard. Another one commented "*I guess that's why they call it the blues* club."

I think that the *Honky cat* is a very unusual breed of cat but a lot of women like them; especially the high society *Honky Tonk women* from *Border Song* who are always in the spotlight of the fashion magazines.

I knew that the cook in the diner would *feed me* without a meal ticket but the diner also bought back some memories to me; some good and some bad.

As I walked into the diner and looked around, I recalled seeing a group of *Mona Lisas and Mad Hatters* sitting in a couple of booths in the diner and *I saw her standing there* at the end of one booth. *I never knew her name* but she was beautiful and she seemed to be *young, gifted and black*.

The cook said "They all belong to the *Rock and Roll Madonna* Dance Troupe but the one standing may not be able to continue travelling with them.

During *the last song* of their rehearsals today, her partner took a *step too far* to the left and slipped and the way that his leg did a *twist* and the *shout* of agony that he gave, she thinks that he must have broken it.

The show must go on and without a partner, she is unable to dance or continue with the troupe.

I have taken over this diner from my father and if I remember correctly, you used to come in here with your father before you moved to the Moon.

Your family moved here to *Your Song* from Earth but your grandfather lived on the Moon so after about two years here, you moved to the Moon. You are the *son of your father.*"

The cook rummaged through some old papers behind the meal ticket box and turned around smiling with a picture from a magazine in his hand and he continued saying "Here, this is the picture of me, my father, your father and you when we reopened the place. It was taken as *Steve redecorates* the final wall with his art work. Look at it; see, I said that you are the *son of your father.*"

Sorry boys, I just got side tracked a little.

I left *Your Song* and caught the *Skyline Pigeon* Intercity Shuttle to Hot Encore and was going to catch the train down to *Crocodile Rock* but before I boarded, I asked to driver if the train stopped at

Crocodile Rock and the driver told me
"*This train don't stop there anymore.*"

In the summertime, Crocodile Rock can
be very good for growing things and in
winter it is a good place for cold storage
without having to freeze anything.

I also wanted to get some water, soil
and vegetation samples so I could
analyze them in my laboratory.

I didn't want to say *goodbye Yellow
Brick Road* Tavern as I had had to do a
few times before when I had to get off at
the train stop before *Crocodile Rock* so I
decided to see if I could get a ferry there
instead.

I saw the *madman across the water* of
the *Yellow River* walking towards the
river vessels as I was walking to *the
bridge* that would take me over to them
and I hurried to try and get the ferry that
he was on but I missed it.

I thought afterwards that I was lucky
that I did miss it because *the one* person
who I didn't want to see me was the
madman.

I caught the next ferry up the river and

got all the samples I needed and got out of there quick.

I left Hot Encore and went to Nubia where I again met with St Peter. I showed him the samples and told him about hearing the strange version of the *song for Guy* and once again I asked "*Where to now St. Peter?* You seem to know where I am supposed to go next."

St Peter told me to do what I was going to do; take the samples back to my lab on *Corona*.

When Corona was first discovered, the Government thought that there was not enough on the planet to sustain a large population so they left it alone but I found the *simple life* very relaxing and rewarding.

I built a small dwelling beside one pyramid shaped mountain and close to *another pyramid* shaped mountain, not too far away, I built my laboratory and as the years have passed, my lab has grown and I now have many scientists, botanists and biologists working on the issue of the green mist.

Originally the mist was clear but because the mist has been tampered with over the years, it has become pale green."

"Mr. Brumby." said Nikita "so are we on the right track?

We had a conference call with all the people out in the field that Daniel set up for us. *Bennie and the Jets* are flying in from *Your Song* immediately and the half of the Brown Dirt Cowboys that are in *Levon* are picking up Little Jeannie and bringing her here before re-joining Captain Fantastic on the bad side of the Moon. Roy Rogers is flying in from Sacrifice and will be joining Captain Fantastic on the bad side of the Moon."

"Daniel! Who's Daniel? Have you boys employed another person without consulting me?" said Mr. Brumby.

"Aw come on dad; you know Daniel. He's been working with *Bennie and the Jets,* you and granddad for many years. There is a lot of mentioning of him and Dan Dare in all your books.

Actually we are waiting for Dan to get

back in contact with us once he has finished his mission.

This green mist has scattered our people all over the Universe and has affected a couple of our females. Tiny Dancer has been badly affected and she is with Rocket Man who is keeping her with him in *Crocodile Rock*.

We all saw what Tiny was like on the monitor and Bennie suggested that we should get Tiny away from Rocket Man as soon as possible as she is in danger. Bennie also asked Daniel to help us.

I wonder where he is because he should be here right now helping us sort through all the messages and information from the conference call." said Harry.

Then Tom said "He must have left the room and he must have walked right through you as you walked in dad."

"That's right." said Nikita "Daniel left the same time as you came into the Boardroom."

"Nobody passed me at all, let alone Daniel." replied Mr. Brumby.

"Are you sure?" questioned Tom "Daniel was here. Bennie sent him back from *Your Song* to help us with this issue.

We'll replay the tapes and recordings, so that you can see for yourself that he was here and know that we have not been affected by this mist."

"Did you say that you still have a couple of my books to read?" said Mr. Brumby.

"Yes dad." said Tom "Why?"

"Well, if you had read them, then you would know that Dan Dare, Daniel and another passenger named James disappeared while on a mission many years ago. Nobody knows what happened.

All we know is that they were heading for Nubia to talk to St. Peter. The radar, on *Your Song,* that was tracking them, had them on the scope and then suddenly they weren't there anymore; just *empty sky*. There were two more crafts in the same vicinity as the boys but no-one saw them." said Mr. Brumby.

Harry said "When you see the replays of the tapes and communications, then you will know that we are not making it up. Little Jeanie was helped to safety by James and Dan Dare just two days ago. You can ask her later on when she gets here."

"That's right." said Nikita "I have often worked with Daniel during our communications and he is the one who set up our systems today, including the old type text recorder and printer that I didn't know we had as well as the monitors. He also told me to set the monitors and sets to five, five one so that we could get good reception from everyone, even if they are on the bad side of the moon."

Mr. Brumby went pale and slumped back into the large chair he was sitting in and very quietly whispered "It can't be. He can't be."

"Mr. Brumby! Are you alright? Would you like me to get you something to drink?" asked Nikita.

"Another coffee would be nice thank you. Now let me watch and listen to those communications and then we'll discuss the communications, what you three have discovered and the results of what I have been working on." replied Mr. Brumby.

After watching the communications Mr. Brumby looked like he had just seen a ghost. He turned to Tom and Harry and said "You were right about Daniel helping you but he is *the one* question that I am not able to give an answer too. Right now, let's get down to our findings. You go first Harry."

"Well." said Harry "I do *believe* that the green mist is a good type of bacteria that has been tampered with. Good bacteria can be used to make Penicillin and other helpful medicines.

The bacteria float around in the air and when a certain type of moisture is introduced to it, it becomes a bad bacterium that covers the universe like a green misty type of rain. That's all I've figured out at this moment.

Am I on the right track?"

"Yes, you are. *Breaking down the barriers* of each bacterium is a long slow process as each of the bacteria has a band of energy around it.

My biologists, bacteriologists, microbiologists and scientists use *band introductions* for each one so that they know which one they are working on and how that particular band works.

As the scientists *come down in time,* they also introduce other substances to the bacterium and with the *introduction* of each new substance; they can monitor the effect that it has on it. They have made very good progress up to now but have not found a way to stop the green mist or its effect on human life.

One of my female researchers became affected by the bacteria and became hostile and possessive of the vials that she was working on. In fact, she even told the head of the biology unit to "Go *grow some funk of your own.*"

As you have already found out that sedated sleep does help clear the affects within three hours; however this is not always the case.

Tiny Dancer is a good subject because when she was talking to you boys, she seemed confused in her way of thinking.

She used the term *goodbye Yellow Brick Road* first, our secret call sign for help, then *Can you feel the love tonight, My baby loves love, Are you ready for love* and *come and get it.*

Then she became kind of depressed and said things like; *Don't let the sun go down on me, My baby left me* and *Don't go breaking my heart. Love is a cannibal* that will eat you up but, with some sort of drug that messes with your mind, *love lies bleeding* in a state of confusion.

I could *go on and on* about what this particular type of bacteria can do if altered in different ways but now is not the time for me to do that.

Now Tom, what have you worked out?"

"I think that I have worked out who the bitch is.

Every time a report came in that the *bitch is back,* it seems that Rocket Man was also in the area of the reported sighting. If he used different substances to alter the appearance of something, then why can't he use something to change his own appearance, even if only for a few hours?

Every time a report of the *bitch is back* came in, it states that she was only there for a short time and then disappeared. It seems to me through reading all these books that Rocket Man wants to become and stay the *forever man*.

You know that if he is trying to manipulate the bacteria to affect everyone in the universe then he is a *stone's throw away from hurtin'* himself because there are always people like us who will try and stop him.

I feel like a bullet wouldn't have any effect on him except to make him hostile towards the person with the gun. The weapons of today would not be any use either because he would have found a way to stop the effect of the particular weapon. Is that what you were trying to work out dad?" replied Tom.

Mr. Brumby replied "Actually Tom, you have worked out much more than I have until now.

Do you remember reading the passage; "Who would think that the bitch could be young gifted and black?

I still remember the first time we met and she said "*Don't let the sun go down on me* because I despise the Midnight Creeper. He will *come down in time* and blow out the *candle in the wind* leaving me with a head full of *sad songs* to get me through the night.

Tonight you will have to catch one of the planes to Reverie and then the train to Logos and walk back from there to the Cottonfields *Country Comfort* Motel, because *this train don't stop there anymore.* You will be glad to say "*goodbye Yellow Brick Road*" once you have reached the motel because you'll hear nothing but whispers coming from the trees whilst you're walking and the trees won't be whispering about the *love of the common people* either.

We all fall in love sometimes but *don't go breaking my heart* because *it's me that you need* to keep you floating down the river of dreams. *It's all in the game* but it's easier to walk away from a man who never died than it is living in Jimmie Rodger's Dream. Yes, *I've seen that movie too* and *I've seen the saucers* in the heels of the wind and I know who travels with their occupants beside the captain & the kid.... The man with the *blue eyes* and everybody gonna know when he is around."

Just before she turned and walked towards the Ladies Room, she gave me a little box and that was the last time I saw her.

I never got to ask her to explain herself so I didn't know what the meaning was to what she had said.

That box contained some white powder and my scientists think that it may be the antidote for the green mist/rain affect.

They are still working on it because the powder contains some substances that are not known to us today, they are from your great grandfather's and grandfather's era.

I also have my geologists and paleontologists working with them in case there are some rocks or soil residue in the substances."

"Wait a minute." said Nikita "that doesn't make sense. If the bitch is Rocket Man and he is responsible for the green mist, why would he give you the antidote way back then?

Also why would he mention the saucers and who flies in them. Rocket Man's *ego* couldn't be that big that he thinks that no-one can touch or stop him.

It's a bit like him thinking that he had *better have a gift* for you and then giving you the *wrong gift* on your birthday and then him *calling it Christmas* and being adamant that *Christmas must be tonight*.

Now I'm confusing myself."

"Yes, that's right. It does seem odd that you may have been given the antidote all those years ago and the green mist has started affecting more people now.

If Rocket Man is the *madman across the water;* could he also be the bitch. I am with you now Nikita. *I can't tell the bottom from the top* of this story.

I feel like I have to stay here until I have worked it out so please *don't let the sun go down on me* until I have." said Harry.

Tom interrupted by saying "Do you want to know *how I know you* could have come to that conclusion, Harry.

Like dad said before; when we read these books we analyze what has been written in the past. Today's world is different. You can notice it more because of the *elaborate lives* that more people live now compared to granddad's era.

Do you think that Rocket Man is going to walk in here and say *"I am your robot?"* I don't think so.

Although he may buy and perhaps eat *rotten peaches* and live in *Crocodile Rock,* a very cold place, I do *believe* that he is of some kind of living form; he may even be human.

Also like Nikita said, we have never really seen his face, so we don't know if he is old or young. He may even be a second, third or fourth generation carrying on a family tradition but who are we to say that he is the bad guy or the bitch.

Dad, do you know where he's from?"

Before their father could answer, Nikita called out "Mr. Brumby, I have a *Rock and Roll Madonna* from the *Mona Lisas and Mad Hatters* Dance Troupe on the monitor. She told me to tell you to *rock me when he's gone*. Do you know what she's on about?"

Mr. Brumby rushed to the monitor and replied "*I'm a natural sinner* but only in the *original sin*. Go ahead *Rock 'N' Roll Madonna;* you can speak to me in safety."

"Mr. Brumby the *Mona Lisas and Mad Hatters* have just arrived here on Earth to start our tour and to go to a *funeral for a friend* of two of the guys. We had just said *good morning Freedom* when we heard sirens nearby and a lot of shouting.

Evidently there was a breakout from the High Security Prison this morning and the escapee made his way to the *Skyline Pigeon* Shuttle where he took one of the cabin crew hostage and said to her "*I'm going home* so *take me to the pilot.*"

Two of the *Grey Seal* Naval Officers, *Donner Pour Donner* and his brother, *Idol* saw what was happening and tackled the escapee killing him.

During the *interviews,* the reporters claimed that the escapee was *Pinball Wizard* and in the note he left hidden under his mattress, he said that he was on his way to visit *Lucy in the sky with Diamonds* on Transvenus and it's where *the king must die* because he tried to *burn down the mission* and then he was going to visit the *madman across the water.*

His final intention was to ambush and kill *Bennie & the Jets* and all your other workers in the field and then come after you and your family and workers.

He then wrote that once he had done all that, *I think I'm going to kill myself.*

If he knew about us *Mona Lisas and Mad Hatters* he would have tried to kill us too. We have a short tour here and I will be glad to say *goodbye Yellow Brick Road* Dance Hall and head back home to my own family and my *Honky cat."*

"Thank you Madonna. Enjoy the rest of your tour especially dancing in the dance hall. Saying *goodbye Yellow Brick Road* Dance Hall will not be easy because of the history of the place and the experience that you will have dancing on that unique floor. *I'm still standing* after dancing on it many, many years ago.

A friend said to me once "*Your sister can't twist but she can rock and roll,* but you are the opposite because you can *twist & shout* but that's all you can do."

I know that your family and your *Honky cat* will be very pleased to see you back home.

Once this tour is over, how long do you have off before you go back into training again for a new dance production?"

Madonna replied "I think that we have three months off before we start rehearsals for the remake of *Hoop Of Fire*. Do you know that it's almost *sixty years on* since the original was performed and the first performance was in *Tickling on Your Song* which is my home town."

"Thank you for contacting me with that good piece of news, I'll let you go now but if you or any of the *Mona Lisas and Mad Hatters* need to contact me and I'm not here; you will be able to talk to one of my sons, Tom or Harry." said Mr. Brumby.

As Mr. Brumby sat down at the big table Tom said "I think that it's time you started telling us about what's going on and what the *Mona Lisas and Mad Hatters* have to do with us?"

Mr Brumby began "It all started back when Danny Bailey passed. Your great grandfather started this agency to try and protect the citizens from violence and crime.

His first team that went out into the field also carried the name of *Bennie and the Jets* and they were all trained at the *Grey Seal* Naval Base.

The government at the time acknowledged your great grandfather's work and ideas and allowed him to proceed.

At first they were called *Bennie & the Yets* but change the name to *Bennie & the Jets* because they seemed to be able to get to different places quite quickly. When people knew that *Bennie and the Jets* were around, they used to say "*Have mercy on the criminal* that they're after." and after a few years, the crime rate fell considerably.

As the years rolled on and the discovery of outer space became a reality and the people moved out there, the Government consulted with your great grandfather about making another team that would also be based somewhere in the universe.

They too were to be trained at the *Grey Seal* Naval Base and on their final day of training your great grandfather went out and hand-picked his other team but there were a few people who he felt would be good as solo agents.

One person who excelled and your great grandfather was going to take personally under his wing was *Johnny B Goode* but one afternoon Johnny never turned up for a very important mission. Concerned, your great grandfather went to his place and found Johnny locked in a large *cage* and very *restless* but when he went over to release Johnny from the *cage,* Johnny screamed out "Go *grow some funk of your own.*

Can you feel the love tonight and if you can *don't go breaking my heart* but please *don't let the sun go down on me* in here."

It took your great grandfather nearly an hour to entice him out and once released all he said before he passed out was *Lucy in the sky with diam...*

He never regained consciousness and passed away not long after that and at his *funeral* his relatives played the *Ballad of the boy in the red shoes* because they said that when he was young he always wore his sister's red sneakers.

Your great grandfather chose Captain Fantastic who was from *Reprise* Valley on *Your Song* as the next leader and a group of men that he said looked like dirty brown cowboys and that's how Captain Fantastic and the Brown Dirt Cowboys were formed.

He chose a female named Alice as a solo agent and because *all the girls love Alice*, she would be able to get information from them quite easily.

Michelle was another female that was recruited and she was a dancer before becoming an agent.

She ended up joining the *Mona Lisas and Mad Hatters* for a while until a *lovesick* fool stabbed her to death whilst they were dancing to a *love song* that the fool called *Michelle's song*.

That's when the *Mona Lisas and Mad Hatters* became involved with the agency as information sources. They have supplied us with a lot of information over the decades because of their travelling."

Nikita interrupted by saying "*Sad songs* can say so much to a listener but *sad songs* can also give you the blues. So *I guess that's why they call it the blues* club when you want to go to a place to hear that kind of music.

Sorry, I didn't mean to interrupt."

"A *travellin' band* also became eyes and ears for us but as *Saturday night's alright for fighting* and drinking; they were not given much information or contact details.

At one time, one of a *travellin' band* members reported that after the band had said *goodbye Yellow Brick Road* Dance Hall, he overheard two guys talking about how they could *burn down the mission* with just a *candle in the wind*.

They didn't say where the mission was so your great grandfather couldn't take any action to stop it. It was then that he moved to the Moon and set our agency up here.

Not long after that, my father joined the agency and we moved to *Your Song*.

It was there that I learned more about the people of this universe and how

Saturday night's alright for them to lose the week day working blues and to get together for a relaxing time with their family and friends.

We eventually moved down here so that my father could be more involved with this agency and recruit more field officers. Rocket Man was a very good agent until he started to change.

Crime started to rise again and that's when the bitch first came to our attention. It seemed that when the *bitch is back* in town, there was also an attempt to *burn down the mission* with a *candle in the wind* and sightings of Rocket Man in the vicinity.

Until recently, the worse time for us was when someone tried to *burn down the mission* in *Border Song* when we were going through many cosmic storms.

I went with my father on that trip and when we boarded the craft, I asked one of the crew to *take me to the pilot* as I knew how he could get around the cosmic storm that we were going to head into because we would have been like a *candle in the wind* and severely blown around.

I know that all pilots are trained for cosmic storms but I don't think that this pilot knew just how severe this storm was going to be."

"Dad." said Tom "you haven't mentioned anything about the green rain yet."

"I was coming to that." said Mr. Brumby "now where was I. Oh yes.

It was during that cosmic storm that the green rain appeared. The *first episode at Hienton* was the first sighting of it and it was during a *funeral for a friend* that some of my other *friends* were attending.

They stated that whist they were listening to the *Ballard of a Well-Known Gun* inside the church someone noticed the green rain through the window and luckily that day everyone was inside under cover.

Border Song was where most women were affected but they only went into a trance for about thirty minutes.

Why they kept saying "*Sorry seems to be the hardest word* to say so *I guess that's why they call it the blues* after a fight. *Sorry seems to be the hardest word* to say so *I guess that's why they call it the blues* after a fight." is beyond everyone; even my scientists today can't explain how the green mist can manipulate a woman's mind into saying things that she has no control over."

Harry chuckled and said "I'd give a million bucks for the recipe that would make a woman say things that she never meant to say or think of."

Tom chuckled to himself until their father said "Boys, this is no laughing matter."

Harry and Tom looked at each other; had another little chuckle and said in unison "*Are we laughing?*"

Their father continued "Other reports of the green mist were sent to us but it was at the time that the *seasons* changed so my father didn't take much notice of them.

It was a couple of weeks later that

I noticed that the *Saturday sun* seem to *shine on through* some strange cloud like mist. I went inside and got my camera and took some shots of the sky.

The following day, I showed a friend of mine who had just become a Nepholograher after becoming a Nephologist, just a year before hand and asked *"Hey Ahab,* would you look at these pictures and tell me what you see. You may have to look closely at them.

A Nephologist is someone who has spent years learning about and completing studies of clouds and a Nepholographer is someone who has the credentials to photograph clouds."

Ahab who couldn't speak fluent English took a closer look and stated "To me looks like a few sun rays *shine through* tail of *shooting star.* No wait; something else here; I go get magnifying glass".

We both took a closer look and Ahab said "This not normal cloud for sky, green no color for sky. What is it? Do you know?"

I told him that I didn't know and we

never saw the green rain again.

The crime rate started climbing again so my father had to recruit more people. This time he recruited some people with diverse knowledge, of different age groups and from different cultures.

Roy Rogers was a young man then but he still had a reputation for getting the tasks done. Many people who saw him about would say "*Have mercy on the criminal* if Roy is after them."

Roy also had many friends on numerous planets and the *talking old soldiers* were his best friends. They have helped him over the years because he has always given them the respect that they deserved.

Roy has also put himself out just to take someone to attend a *funeral for a friend* and he stayed with them otherwise they couldn't have gone.

Roy lived on *Your Song* for a while but when he had to *kiss the bride* at his cousin's wedding, he felt like his heart was the flame of the *candle in the wind* that had just been blown out.

Roy didn't know it at the time but he was in a *three way love affair*. She was his *true love* but she got engaged to his cousin.

Roy found out later that she was often in *American triangle* love affairs and would go around *breaking hearts*.

One day Roy's cousin caught his wife with someone else and he told her "*I don't wanna go on with you like that* anymore. *Don't go breaking my heart* like you did to Roy, besides there is *something about the way you look tonight* that makes me wonder, how long have you been cheating on me.

Saturday night's alright for me to walk away from you so you don't need to make excuses for your behavior anymore."

Now as for Rocket Man, none of my relatives knew very much about him; where he was born; when he was born or where he actually lived.

It seemed that he was always travelling."

ROCKET MAN'S STORY

"That's right." said Rocket Man as he walked into the Boardroom "I am always travelling all over this Universe and that is why I am always called Rocket Man but the *madman across the water,* as you call him, was my father.

My grandfather gave me the name of Robert Guy Mann. He changed my surname just after he rescued me when I was a very young child. *I know the truth* and now I think that it's time that you all get to know it too.

As you are aware of most of my grandfather's past and what happened up to the time my father got sick and was given some medicine to save his life.

My grandfather told me many times that my father recovered slowly and as he did he became a very *spiteful child* and a *whipping boy* for all the other boys who lived at the nearby mission.

Eventually he became so angry that he would do everything he could to *burn down the mission* in every place that he went to.

He used to tell my grandfather that to *burn down the mission* and watch it burn was just like watching the *candle in the wind* flicker and then regain its shine and power again.

Dad was in *Philadelphia Freedom* shopping for the latest fashion from the *Emperor's New Clothes* range of men's wear when he met my mom who was buying a *dark diamond* pendant.

They saw each other often and married six months later and moved quite often to different places in the universe. I don't think that mom knew what dad was really like because he always told her a *hard luck story* to make her feel sorry for him.

I was *made in England* on Earth during one of his trips and I was born in the *foreign fields* near *Fanfare* an outer suburb of Middlesex Freedom, on Urallas.

Mom had just said *good morning Freedom* when I arrived earlier than what was expected but dad couldn't take mom to the mission for help because he had just tried to *burn down the mission.*

A *sweet painted lady* was passing and stopped to help mom and dad and took my parents to the nearest train station where dad bought tickets for *Indian Sunset,* the place where his uncle lived.

On the train my father asked the guard as to how long before they would reach *Indian Sunset* and the guard replied "*This train don't stop there anymore* because not enough passengers used the station.

Most people who want to travel there usually get off at *Te Dare* and catch the bus back the following day and *Saturday night's alright* for staying there because the place was very quiet and trouble free."

My mother told my father's dad that after saying *goodbye Yellow Brick Road* Hotel and boarding the bus, she overheard someone sitting in front of them say "*Where to now St Peter?*

I think that whoever is trying to *burn down the mission* in just about every town should be whipped and thrown in jail before they trap and kill somebody who is still inside it. Then again, if the person who was trying to *burn down the mission* was really serious in doing it, you would think that they would use something stronger than leaving a *candle in the wind* that could be easily blown out."

St Peter answered "Just *up around the bend* is the home base and terminals of the *Skyline Pigeon* Intercity Shuttles and we will be stopping there to pick up some extra passengers.

Since God invented girls, we have also been teaching some of them to live in our ways; *Susie,* Alice and *Chloe* have been living and learning at the *Circle Of Life* Centre for the past ten years.

All the girls love Alice so she stays at the centre to welcome and settle in all the new girls, Chloe has successfully finished the *Recover Your Soul* Program and *she's waiting* for us at the terminal. We will be there for about an hour as that will allow all the people who intend to travel on, to get on the bus.

I will know more of where we will be going after I have spoken to her.

Susie is proceeding in her studies a lot better than she was because when she first joined us, she had shed *too many tears* and still felt the *weight of the world* on her shoulders.

She was found standing over an unknown dead body in a state of shock, holding a gun and a note. Even though the gun had not been fired, the note said "This is *my father's gun* and it sings a *Texan love song* because *mama can't buy you love* anymore. I am a *long way from happiness* now because *love lies bleeding* at my feet.

There was a *word in Spanish* that no one could translate so we felt that it could have been from their ancient language."

Susie still can't remember what happened in her past and *time has told me* never to force someone to remember any sort of traumatic experiences."

Grandfather told me that when mom and dad reached *Indian Sunset,* dad's uncle was on a trip to *Your Song* collecting special supplies for his experiments and medicinal purposes and arrived back several days later.

Dad became extremely interested in one of his uncle's experiments and decided to use me as a living specimen.

Mom did everything she could to stop him but he would *wrap her up* in an enormous piece of cloth and force her to drink a cloudy liquid that would calm her down.

Mom took *one day at a time* and waited for the right time to leave; taking me back to her parents place in *Philadelphia Freedom*. She also contacted grandfather, dad's dad, begging him to come and get me before dad could find us. Dad found us quicker than mom thought he would but he didn't know that grandfather was arriving that afternoon.

I was really *too young* to know what was going on but back at grandfather's place, I remember that he used to sing me the *song for Guy* that he had written for his son many years before.

One morning grandfather came in and pulled me out of bed and carried me *up around the bend* of the *Yellow River* where we boarded a *Dreamboat* that was giving its passengers *candy by the pound*.

I was only allowed to have a couple of pieces but when we reached the *Skyline Pigeon* Intercity Shuttle, grandfather said to the head of the cabin crew staff as he handed me over to her "*Take me to the pilot;* it's a matter of urgency."

I never did find out what grandfather said to the pilot and I never saw him again. I was placed in a mission in *Fanfare* for a few years until someone again tried to *burn down the mission* that I was in.

As I was now at the age where I could work and I knew that it was *sixty years on* since one of my relatives had worked for this agency, I decided to apply for a position and I gained employment with you.

Being able to travel for you meant that I could also try to find my family as well.

It was during the third trip back to *Philadelphia Freedom* that I found out that my mother was addicted to the cloudy water that my father had given her and whilst she was sitting on the ledge of an upstairs open window, she said to her mother "*Look ma, no hands.*" and just as my father walked through the door she fell backwards out the window.

Evidently, dad rushed over to the opened window and looked down before saying "My *love lies bleeding* on the path below. *Someone saved my life tonight* by falling out of a window and now I am free to carry on with my work without having to worry about you."

He turned to his mother-in-law and said "At least *I'm still standing* so *don't let the sun go down on me* just yet. I know that *sorry seems to be the hardest word* to say and I am *sorry* for the loss of your daughter but when *love is dying* no *country love song* will bring it back.

I have set the timer on the old clock so please *tell me when the whistle blows.*

You had better do something about her body and don't expect to see me at the funeral because I won't be there; I won't even go to a *funeral for a friend.*"

I personally think that she was *better off dead* rather than being a living specimen for my father.

I also found out that he had something to do with the bacteria that travelled in the clouds.

This particular strain of bacteria was an extension of what his uncle was working on and when it was released from the clouds it became a pale green mist that had certain effects on women.

The newest strain also had effects on children so I realized that he had to be stopped before he could release a mist that would affect everyone.

My father could then take control over them just like he told his father he wanted to do. Grandfather once told me that my father had told him "*I'm going to be a teenage idol* first but *I just can't wait to be king* of the universe."

On my travels with your agency and my search for my father, I met Tiny Dancer briefly and I fell in love with her.

I had been in love just once before but that ended badly because of my father and I swore that I'm *never gonna fall in love again* but when *I saw her standing there* in the doorway of the *Screw You* River Blues Club, I couldn't help myself.

I knew I was on *shakey ground* when I approached her as she was saying to the *Honkey Tonk Women,* each with their *Honky cat,* from *Border Song "I guess that's why they call it the blues.*

To some people *sad songs say so much* and to other people, *sad songs* can sound just like a *love song* or two and *I want love* all the time from the *love of the common people* who love listening to the blues.

Can you feel the love tonight that most of the people here have for the blues? Every day I say to someone *"Don't let the sun go down on me* until I have reached a Blues Club somewhere in this universe."

I was not that familiar with the blues nor did I have the love for it like she had, so I knew that it would be *easier to walk away* from Tiny before I got too involved with her.

You gotta love someone but all I really wanted to do was walk up to Tiny and *wrap her up* with all my love; however *I want love* too and I wasn't sure if she would love me back.

I left the club thinking to myself "*I guess that's why they call it the blues* because when *you're so static* like I am with music, the *love of the common people* who love music will always win out.

I also had to ask myself "*are you ready for love* right now or will my *gypsy heart* and the need to find my father and somehow change this *circle of life* that I have now, be like the *slave* that wants to be like the *high flying bird* that is not surrounded by a *cage* or like a *candle in the wind* that can be put out at any moment.

I'm still standing and I'm *blessed* with the *memory of love* that my mother gave me. *Love's got a lot to answer for* and so has my father, who really was the *madman across the water."*

I saw a *Honky cat* slip into a doorway just as St Peter stepped out from it and turn in my direction.

He stopped suddenly in front of me, looked me up and down and said "Robert Guy Mann. I remember you from the mission that your grandfather sent you too for safety. You have grown so tall but you have that empty look in your eyes, just like your mother had and an anguished look on your face, just like the one I saw on your grandfather's face when I last saw him. Are you alright? Where are you heading too?

I wanted to *yell help; I think I will kill myself* if I can't sort my head out and *if there is a God in heaven* please help me find a way, *don't let the sun go down on me* just yet.

I think St Peter must have known what was going through my head because he said "Come let's walk to the *Tinderbox* Café and we can talk over a coffee. There are some things that you should know about your family and now that you are older it would be easier for you to accept."

Over coffee St Peter said "I know your father and he wasn't *born bad* but he has become like a sly *fox*.

In the beginning, he tried to make the medicines like his uncle used to make from good bacteria but when your mother became ill with Bacterial Social Disease, he became obsessed in trying to find a cure.

His uncle told him "Go and *grow some funk of your own* that you can use in your experiments." and he did.

The disease she had was like an old time disease that killed many people on Earth and that was called Yellow Fever.

I don't know too much about it, but I *believe* it was carried by mosquitoes that drank stagnant water where the bacteria had landed.

The bacteria was formed into Yellow Fever after the mosquitoes had ingested the water and then passed it on to humans through a mosquito bite. The mosquito injected something into the skin of the human to make it easier for them to draw blood from the human. The injected liquid with the bad bacteria in it then entered the blood stream of the human, making them ill and most times killing them.

Other factors must be taken into account because Yellow Fever was contagious and spread quickly, killing many thousands of people in a matter of a short time.

Malaria was also one other disease that was carried by mosquitos and passed on to humans through the mosquito's blood drawing process. Malaria, if not treated properly, would damage or destroy organs in the human that could finally kill them. Mosquito bites were usually harmless to humans.

Your father found that by using bacteria in another way, he could help relieve the pain and symptoms that your mother had by mixing the bacteria formula with water to make a drink which he gave her but he kept making it stronger and stronger until she could no longer think clearly and fell to her death.

If he had kept giving it to her in a weaker dose, then your mother may have lived until a cure was found. Yellow Fever, Malaria, and a few more diseases like them are not around on Earth anymore so I won't carry on with that story.

I should not be saying this but I think that your mother was *better off dead* rather than living the life of a living guinea pig that your father was using her for. I know that your father has experimented on other people and has killed a couple of people.

I only know of this because I presided over a *funeral for a friend* who told me that too many tears had been shed by what your father was doing and he must be stopped. Nobody can prove what he is doing because the people who know are dead and the other people can't prove it yet.

When your mother passed *I should have sent roses* but I didn't want your father knowing that I knew what had happened.

She said to me once '*Don't let the sun go down on me* while *I'm still standing*. I need to find my son first.

My baby loves lovin' and he needs plenty of it but I want to be the one to give it to him. I want to find him so that I can tell him that I'm sorry for letting him go and to say *come back baby* and spend time with me."

I looked out the window and watched the *street kids* doing the *street boogie* before looking back at St Peter and telling him all that I knew. I also told him that I wanted to find my father and talk to him.

St Peter said "Your father has become more than the *madman across the water*. This is the time of year where he will say *Goodbye Yellow Brick Road* Motel and head back to *Crocodile Rock* by a *Skyline Pigeon* shuttle.

He will try and find some female to accompany him back and she will be his next experimental guinea pig.

If you do find him at home, be very careful about accepting anything from him as he may try to harm or even kill you because you are not the *son of your father* but the son of your mother who was very kind and gentle.

I'm still standing because he hasn't found me yet and *I don't wanna go out like that;* poisoned and have to have my friends attending a *funeral for a friend.*

If you need me at all, I will be saying *good morning Freedom* and visiting the *Pinball Wizard* and *Razor Face* in the *Philadelphia Freedom* High Security Prison, for the next three days asking God to *have mercy on the criminal,* and then I will be going to *Fanfare* to *kiss the bride* at a friend's wedding.

That will be a very lavish affair because *all the girls love Alice* and they will all want to be bridesmaids. Even *all the young girls love Alice* because she is a great teacher at her school.

After that I will be going to *Karmatron* to oversee the final stages of the building our new mission and to dedicate it.

Even now, after *sixty years on*, someone still tries to *burn down the mission* in every town across the universe using a *candle in the wind*. The last time they did a pretty good job because they used a flammable liquid as well.

I don't wanna go on with that story anymore because it's time for me to leave."

St Peter finished his coffee and left, leaving me to ponder over what he had told me. I knew that he was right; my father was dangerous and had to be stopped. But how?

I walked back to the club and stood outside and listened to the music for a short while and as I walked away I thought "Tiny, *I've been loving you* for so such a short time but I have only just realized how much I do care for you.

I can't steer my heart clear of you but *are you ready for love?*

Sad songs do say so much to the heart and they can get you down so *I guess that's why they call it the blues*.

If I ever get the opportunity to talk with you, I will tell you how I feel and ask you to go out with me but first I have to deal with my father."

I made my way back to Hot Encore and stayed in the *Holiday Inn* for a few days and after saying *goodbye Yellow Brick Road* and *Grey Seal Street,* I ran into *Lucy in the sky with diamonds* and she told me that she had overheard a plot to kill her husband, the King of Transvenus and was trying to get in touch with the agency because she had no idea why *the king must die*.

I told her not to worry about that because I would do it for her but I became aware of an odd smell and knew that my father was nearby.

I hurried down to the *Slow Rivers* Express Way and caught the next boat to *Crocodile Rock*. The captain said something to one of the crew and then turned to the person at the wheel and shouted "*Slow down Georgie, if the river can bend* then we have to be able to bend too but if we're going too fast then we'll just go crashing into the river bank.

I'm a natural sinner but *I'm still standing* and I want to stay that way. I don't want the *Island girl pickin' on* me tonight if I walk into the *Country Comfort* Diner with a broken arm or leg."

As I walked up the back path of our house, dad called out "Hi son, what are you doing here?" and went inside. I followed him in and took off my helmet. I told him that I was on a mission to find out who was causing trouble in that area. I think he knew why I was really there.

He walked into the kitchen and returned a few minutes later with a couple of orange drinks and he handed one to me.

He started looking for something and went back outside. I was just about to take a sip of my drink when I remembered what St Peter had told me and I quickly exchanged glasses, just like they did in the olden day movies back on Earth.

Dad came back in carrying some pruning shears in his hand and downed his glass of orange drink.

He then yelled "What did you do; did you swap glasses on me? Do you know what you've done?

I told my father that *I'm going to be a teenage idol* and then king but you seem to think that the *king must die*. Well, you have killed my dream.

I know that *sorry seems to be the hardest word* to say and I'm not sorry for anything I've done, but you will be sorry for what you have done. You will get the blame for everything; Rocket Man.

Your grandfather did the right thing when he hid you from me and your mother paid the price for letting him do it."

Dad went pale and dropped down on a chair and then said "*Saturday night's alright for fighting,* drinking and to say *oodbye Yelow Brick Road* and come home but *please don't let the sun...*" and he died.

I left him where he was but with a note saying "*Sorry seems to be the hardest word* to say in *Philadelphia Freedom* and *I guess that's why they call it the blues* because the *bitch is back* like a *candle in the wind* so *I think I'm gonna kill myself.*" and slipped out the back way and came back here to the Moon.

I was really going to go back to *Your Song* but after getting your communication I had to ask a cabin crew to *take me to the pilot* so she could alter her course and bring me here to the Moon.

When you told me about Tiny Dancer, I became upset because of the way I felt about her.

A blonde haired man did bring her to a friend's place where I was staying and he had also told Tiny that it was my father who was the *madman across the water* and not me. I took her back to *Crocodile Rock* so that we both would walk in and find my father dead and looking like he had killed himself.

I still hadn't finished dealing with my father's friends who were helping him and it wasn't safe for the word to get out about my father. No one would have believed me so I contacted St Peter, explained everything to him and asked "*Where to now St Peter?*"

He suggested that I keep Tiny with me for a few more days until he could meet up with us and come here.

I couldn't think of a way to keep Tiny in a cold place for very long and that's when I remembered that the juice from *rotten peaches* could sedate a person and keep their mind unclear, so that's why I was giving Tiny the cloudy water to drink.

I knew that it would not hurt her or cause her any lasting damage but I couldn't let her tell you about what she knew when you contacted us. Also that was why I became agitated when Little Jeannie mentioned those gentlemen's names.

They are dangerous men and I can't take them on, on my own so I will need your help."

"With all the information that we have read about Rocket Man and all that we are now learning about you; how can we *believe* what you're telling us is true. As far as we know, you could be the *son of your father* and following in his footsteps?" questioned Harry.

"Yes." said Tom "if what you say is true; why didn't you bring Tiny Dancer back with you?

Over the past few days, we've had to jump *into the old man's shoes* so what's to say that you haven't jumped into your old man's shoes as well."

"Oh, but I have brought Tiny back with me and she is waiting outside stroking a *Honky cat* and with a close friend of mine.

She is completely safe and back to her old self. I didn't want to put both my friends in danger by bringing them in here just in case you thought that *Saturday night's alright for fighting*. There are a lot of things that you don't know yet and a *young man's blues* don't disappear overnight.

I needed help and had to take *one day at a time* so I turned to a friend whom I met whilst I was walking down *Grey Seal Street* on *Your Song*. We had a really good talk and he told me about my parents and what happened in my past and then he said "*Let me be your car* and together we can change your *circle of life.*" replied Rocket Man.

"I think that your story is a bit like a *candle in the wind* and at any moment it will go out. I worked with your father and I knew that the *first episode at Hienton* after the tragic death of your mother followed by the *funeral of a friend* set your father's thinking and life in a downward spiral.

Your father did attend your mother's funeral; however, he stood in a concealed place where he thought no-one could see him but I noticed that he was there.

I also know that your mother loved him very much in the beginning and had often told him "*Don't go breaking my heart* and *don't let the sun go down on me* unless you are there with me."

I was also there to *kiss the bride* on the day that they were married and so was Bennie from *Bennie & the Jets.*

My wife and I nearly didn't make the wedding because after a week of our well earned holiday, we had to say *goodbye Yellow Brick Road Holiday Inn,* which was damaged beyond repair by a cosmic storm a year later.

Bennie and the Jets were in *Border Song* investigating the report that someone had tried to *burn down the mission* with a *candle in the wind,* a piece of rope and some flammable liquid.

They discovered that a young Neanderthal man named *Scaffold* was responsible and he was taken back to his people who dealt with his crime by their laws. It was also revealed that during a search of the young man's quarters, the elders had found a plan to *shoot down the moon* in his own hand *writing.*

I'm a natural sinner, as well as all of you are and sometime in our life we have to pay the consequences for our *original sin* but we are rewarded in some way for the good we do for others, it is the way of the Natural Law; however *if you were me,* would you believe your story.

Who is this friend that you trust so much that you would bring them to this office; that you would put our lives and Tiny's life in danger for?" asked Mr. Brumby.

TWO MORE STORIES

The Boardroom door opened and standing in front of them were Tiny Dancer and St Peter.

"St Peter." whispered Mr. Brumby and then in a louder voice he asked "why didn't you tell me that you knew and was helping Rocket Man. It would have been a lot easier to solve this green mist mystery?"

St Peter looked at Mr. Brumby and replied "I tell you *all that I'm allowed* to tell you at the time. Telling you about everything would have been a breach in confidentiality."

Nikita rushed over to Tiny and asked how she was.

Tiny said "Before you go on any further St Peter, would you let me tell them my story so that what you say will join everything together?

St Peter nodded yes to Tiny.

Tiny began by saying to Rocket Man "Robert, that drink you kept giving me was very nice but it didn't have the effect on me as you thought it did, I pretended that it did.

You see, the only thing that has ever affected me was the green mist and I don't know why it did.

Where I come from, every person born is born with immunity against just about everything that can harm us or make us a *slave* to something or someone.

I had to keep up the pretext so that I could listen and observe all that was happening around me without suspicion.

I knew, before the blue eyed man who left me in front of your friend's door, that you were not the person responsible for the green mist; that it was your father's doing.

The blue eyed man told me a lot of things about you that I will tell you later. He also told me that his name was Daniel and he gave me everlasting protection from the green mist, no matter what form it came in or to whom it may affect.

This was just in case your efforts to stop your father failed and I would be able to stop him myself.

DBR wrote and sang many beautiful and meaningful songs but I have never heard a blues song that really sounded as good as the *Song for Guy.* You are very lucky to have such a beautiful song written for you.

Sorry seems to be the hardest word for most people to say; however, it isn't hard for you, because when you said it to me many times, you said it from your heart.

Robert, remember, *mama can't buy you love* but you receive it from many people in many different ways.

When Daniel rescued me that night, I thought "*Someone saved my life tonight, I'm still standing* and I'm standing still in front of this door with a meal ticket in my hand." but when I saw you I had to *come down in time* and knew that the *love of the common people* is better than what I had expected.

I said that I had to *come down in time* because my real home planet of *Reprise* is a few light years ahead of yours in this universe.

I heard many *sad songs* and love songs

that I loved; *I guess that's why they call it the blues* or rather I should call it blues music. It was as *easy as life* on my home planet for me to settle into your universe because of some of the similarities that we share.

At first, because of the good life I had had at home, my compassion for others was not very tolerant but *I must have lost it on the wind* as I got caught *all up in it* and became more involved with the agency and through what I had learned from my friends.

I met Mr. Brumby Senior on one of his trips to *Border Song* and we became good friends and I joined the agency. I know that this is a different story that you may had read or even heard but he didn't want people to know too much about our friendship. *It's all in the game* of confidentiality.

I even met his wife on a few occasions and we taught each other about our ways of life and our friendship was more than a *candle in the wind;* it was like a mother/daughter bond.

When she passed I went to the *funeral of a friend* but I knew that she had only left her earthly body here, her soul went back home and she became a *spirit in the sky* to watch over each and every one that she loved.

Then Mr. Brumby took over from where his father had left it and built up the agency to where it is now and soon Tom and Harry will take it over and hopefully expand it some more.

I know that the law enforcers on each planet have immense respect for what your past relatives have done and what your father is doing now so you boys will have all the help that you need as long as you respect the law enforcers and their laws.

It's all in the game between the criminals and law enforcers to see who will win and I know that you and the law enforcers will win every time.

When I first arrived here on the Moon, I decided to take a trip to see if I was interested in living here.

I am not as old as you think because I

knew Mr. Brumby Senior and his wife and don't forget that I had *come down in time;* any way it was Mr. Brumby's wife who suggested that I be trained as a freelance agent.

On my first investigative trip to find out who tried to *burn down the mission,* I caught a train to *Mellow* but I was told that *this train don't stop there anymore* but if I got off at Island Junction the *Island girl* who attends the station will arrange for me to get to Mellow. I thanked the man and asked him to *tell me when the whistle blows* so I know where I was to get off.

The best thing about that train ride was that I didn't have to ask someone to *take me to the pilot* where I would have lots of explaining to do.

These days if you have to ask someone to *take me to the pilot,* all you do is show them your credentials and they are more than willing to divert from their normal flight path.

I then went to *Your Song* and I found it to be a place where I could live so I bought myself a hollow or apartment as you would call it on *Blue Avenue* and became interested in your kind of music; especially the blues.

The music is interesting to me as it can either make you feel sad or it can make you feel good but *I guess that's why they call it the blues*. I *don't let the sun go down on me* anywhere I am until I find a place that plays the blues music because for me it's like *someone saved my life tonight* and allowed me to forget all my troubles for a while."

Robert asked "If you already knew about me and my father, why didn't you tell me so that I didn't have to do to you what I did. It would have been easier if I was able to get your help?"

"Daniel asked me to not say anything because he knew about your father's friends and knew if they found out what you had done to your father, they would have come looking for you and tried to kill you.

I'm still standing and so are you but I could be standing here alone if you knew what I was told. Your father's friends would have thought that I was just an experimental female and would have left me alone.

I would have been able to assist you or rescue you if the need had been there.

I need you to turn to your childhood and remember what your mother went through and forgive her for getting you away from your father. This universe would have be an awful place to live in, in the future if your father had gotten away with his plans and now you have changed that.

Your father is *better off dead* and so are his friends and you are the only one that can see that proper justice is done on them. If you are going to back down now and let those men slip away from what they deserve then *I don't want to go on with you like that."*

Nikita, would it be possible for me to sit down and get a drink of cold clear water please?"

Mr. Brumby slumped back in his chair and said "Well, that is something new;

I never knew that about my parents. Dad has not written that in any of his books. I wonder what else we don't know about him.

St Peter, I know that you keep a lot of what people say to you in confidence, but is there anything else about my father that you can tell us that we don't know?"

St Peter said "Now everyone take a seat as I have something to tell you.

When I was very young I lived in a very isolated town called *Seasons* that was fifty miles inland from the old small mining town of *Salvation* on *Your Song*. I'm sorry to say that neither place is there anymore. There used to be an old saying that *Saturday night's alright for fighting* the weekday blues away and it was and still is.

One Saturday night there was a wedding being celebrated between Alice, *all the girls love Alice* because she was so kind, and Trevor.

A fellow named Ziros *Honky Cat* Rav was also in love with Alice but he was so switched on that you would think that he was running on *electricity*. Just as the groom was about to *kiss the bride;* Ziros *Honkey Cat* Rav burst into the mission very angry.

He walked down the aisle to Alice and shouted "I'm *the one* that you're supposed to marry, not him. *Can you feel the love tonight,* especially the *love of the common people* who are here now?

Their love is nothing more than a *candle in the wind* that will be extinguished when they are through with you.

I cry at night, I fall apart and *I go to extremes* because *I want love,* your love but if your love is going to be like a *candle in the wind,* well, *I don't wanna go on with you like that. We all fall in love sometimes* but *when I think about love,* I think of you and I ask myself "*Where have all the good times gone?*"

There's *something about the way you look tonight* that is keeping me in *my kind of hell* and I'm not going to stay there without you.

Please *don't go breaking my heart*

again and *don't let the sun go down on me* without you in my arms."

I don't know what happened next because I woke up in the *empty garden*. I knew that Ziros *Honky Cat* Rav wanted to stop the wedding and I knew there had been a struggle; but to *burn down the mission* with all the people inside was crazy.

I started to *run* back to town to raise the alarm when I ran into *Bennie and the Jets* who went to the mission but it was too late to save many of the townsfolk, my parents and Alice. Ziros also died in the mission fire.

Bennie from *Bennie and the Jets* called me *Saint* Peter because he said that I was a little hero and took me to a mission on *Your Song*. That's how I got the name St Peter. During my years at several missions, I became interested in many things and I also *signed sealed delivered* my love and life to God and to do service for him.

It was during my travels *all across the Havens* that I met Robert and his grandfather, who told me about the relationship of Robert's parents.

The pilot of the shuttle that brought Robert to me passed on a letter that informed me of the danger that Robert was in if his father found him. I knew a little about Rocket Man, Robert's father, but this news was surprising.

Someone had tried to *burn down the mission* in *Sacrifice* so I took Robert there as he would be safe and I kept in regular contact with him because he was a troubled young man.

He would often asked questions to which I knew most of the answers but I could only tell him *all that I'm allowed* to tell him.

He learned about his father and a little about what he had done to his grandfather and once he was old enough, he left the mission to seek out his father.

I was glad that he joined your organization because I was still able to keep in contact with him and find out what he had learned so I could direct him in the right direction without him asking more questions.

Once we get this issue over with, I will be able to give more information to Robert and to you Mr. Brumby, Tom, Harry and Nikita.

It is *sixty years on* since I lost my parents and my travels will slowly diminish because it's nearly time for me to retire permanently to Val Hala.

Mr. Brumby, your grandfather gave me some information for you that I was to pass on to you either after he had passed or until it was the right time for me to tell you.

You learned yourself about the green mist and that was one of the things I was to tell you about; however, when you asked for my help I began helping you and gave you the extra information that I had from your father.

He had said to me "*Don't let the sun go down on me* for the final time until I have told you all that I know so that you can pass it on to my son and grandsons."

His final words to me were "*Here's to the next time* when we'll meet in heaven."

Now Robert, I have informed *Bennie and the Jets,* Roy Rogers and Captain Fantastic and the Brown Dirt Cowboys that you are not the person who they think you are and that you are here with me. I also informed them that Tiny Dancer was also with us and that she was safe and well.

They should be here in about thirty minutes with Little Jeannie and Carla and then we will discuss how we are all going to sort out this issue about your father's contacts.

United we stand and we should be able to capture them all whilst they are together. I hope that that is alright with you Mr. Brumby?"

Before Mr. Brumby could answer, Nikita said "I had better go and get a couple of pots of coffee ready and nip to the store next door and get some more supplies.

I'll bet that all the boys will be hungry and thirsty....

That is, if it is safe for me to go outside."

St Peter replied "It's perfectly safe now for you to *go out and get it.* The sun is fully up so say *good morning freedom* when you walk out the doors.

Maybe Tiny would like to help you. A little bit of female company would be good for her now and Little Jeannie and Carla will be here with the boys soon."

"Dad." called Tom "*Lady D'Arbanville* and *Lady Samantha* would like to talk to you. It's something about *Lucy in the sky with diamonds pickin' on* the *Island girl.*"

"Tom would you please apologize to Lady D'Arbanville and inform her that we are all in an urgent meeting that could take up the rest of the day; however if it is not very urgent, then we will try to get back to her later today.

Actually, tell her that she can talk to you about the issue because I have semi-retired. I think that I should let you boys take extra control of the agency before I really do retire.

St Peter, I am going to let you inform

the other field officers of what is going on and you can put your suggestions forward first on how we can end this issue quickly. No doubt you have a brilliant and easy plan just like Daniel would have had." said Mr. Brumby.

"Yes, I do have a brilliant plan and I think it will succeed without any trouble or bloodshed." replied St Peter.

"Pray tell us your plan." said Bennie as he walked through the door followed by the Jets, Little Jeanie, Carla and Captain Fantastic and the Brown Dirt Cowboys.

Captain Fantastic said "Roy is coming up with the ladies as they needed a helping hand.

He told Little Jeannie and Carla to come up with us."

Little Jeannie looked over to the Jets who were together looking at the old type text recorder and said "Where's Daniel. I wanted to make sure that he wasn't James who rescued me?"

The door opened just as St Peter was about to ask Little Jeannie about Daniel and James.

As *Grimsby* cleared some room on the big table for the pots of coffee and the trays of food that was being brought in, he said "You always know how to *feed me* when I come here."

Bennie replied "Now we're not here for a social gathering. We have to work out a plan on how to catch those other gentlemen. St Peter you said you had a plan; would you like to tell us all about it."

"I have discussed this with Tiny and Robert and they also think that it will work.

Border Song has a *Holiday Inn* Blues Club that many people attend and Robert will pretend to be his father and contact his friends asking them to meet him there. He'll tell them that *Saturday night's alright* for the meeting as nobody will take any notice of them coming into the club.

Tiny has agreed and I hope that Little Jeannie and Carla will too, that the three ladies go into the club like they were friends just out for the evening and will sit at a table next to Robert. If I know the men, they will want to buy the ladies a drink and that will get them to the same table.

Little Jeannie you will have to *bite your lip* if they start talking the wrong way until they are safely *signed sealed delivered* to the Enforcement Agency and are in jail. You can then have your say and they will *cry to heaven* for help but an *empty sky* will be the only answer that they will get at that time

I know that all you boys and the ladies were trained at the *Grey Seal* Naval Base, so I would like four of you men to act as waiters in the club for a few hours to be back up for Robert and the ladies.

Bennie and the Jets will stay out the front just in case the men decide to leave early and they can be apprehended.

Roy, Grimsby, Gulliver and a few other Brown Dirt Cowboys will be enjoying the entertainment from the side deck and Captain Fantastic and the rest of the Brown Dirt Cowboys will cover the back entrance into the kitchen.

Roy, if they do come your way then play them the *Ballad of a Well Known Gun* and let them know that you're not a *candle in the wind.*

If the men discover our plan to capture them and each decides to leave by a different exit then there will be a party waiting to greet them when they step outside.

I know that each of these men can be dangerous; however I don't think that they would want to take us all on by themselves. *United we stand* and together we can apprehend them very easily.

Robert made the suggestion that one of the waiters could slip a few drops of the rotten peaches nectar into their drinks as that will calm them down but I'm not sure about that because we won't know if they are immune against it.

What do you think of my plan and has anyone else got something different to offer?" said St Peter.

"I think that's a great idea. *I guess that's why they call it the blues* club and that is exactly what these so called gentlemen are going to get; the blues for the rest of their lives if they live.

The Law Enforcers may think that their crimes are so bad that they will be put into a permanent sleep and it will be just like a *candle in the wind* being blown out by a gentle breeze.

What do you think Benny?" said Mansfield.

Benny replied "I am not sure yet, let me think it over for a while. What if those gentlemen realize that Robert is not his father? They might take him and the females as hostages so that any attempt to capture them could mean the death of one or all of them.

I know that *united we stand* and *Saturday night's alright for fighting* but I wouldn't want to see any of our people getting hurt."

Carla said "I am supposed to be a teacher, so I am a heck lot stronger than any *candle in the wind*.

You're right, *Saturday night is alright for fighting* and I would prefer a decent fight where I can have it legally. I can't fight too well with children because I'm not allowed to."

Everyone just looked at Carla in disbelief over what she had just said.

Carla looked back at them and said *"If the river can bend* then so can I.

I'm not like the *sweet painted lady* who just says to you *"Can you feel the love tonight* and if you can then *don't go breaking my heart* by not doing something about it."

Yes, *I want love* and the love of a good fight with those men will do me good. Any way it has been a long time since I have been able to let my hair down and let off some steam."

Little Jeannie looked at the guys faces and said smiling "Do any of you want to take Carla on?

If you think that *Saturday night's alright for fighting* then you should go and ask some of the men in *Border Song* who have thought that they could make out easily with her.

One man asked her "*Lady what's tomorrow* morning going to be like with you. *Can you feel the love tonight* because I can and *I want love* from you?"

Carla looked down at the man on the ground and said "*I'm still standing* here so my tomorrow is looking great but you are going to have a lot of explaining to do when people ask about your split lip and black eye."

As she walked away from the guy on the ground she picked up a *Honky cat* and whispered in its ear "*I guess that's why they call it the blues* club because he will be leaving with the blues in more ways than one."

Medley took a few steps back from Carla and said "*Not me.* I don't want to fight with her. Actually, I have seen Carla in action.

We had just left this little back wood hick town near the *Yellow River* when a *slave* came running up to her and cried softly "*Someone saved my life tonight* when they had a few words with my master.

She asked him "*Can I put you on* a train to *Theme* Valley. If they tell you that *this train don't stop there anymore* then say to them, "*tell me when the whistle blows* for the next station that you're stopping at and I'll get off there."

She must have said something else to him because he got so scared and released all his slaves; the first being the ones he was going to whip just for fun and then hid himself in his cellar.

We would like to find and thank that woman because now we can all say *good morning freedom* every day and stop living in fear of being whipped for the rest of our lives."

Carla, being a teacher, knew that Theme Valley was where all the slave masters ended up after being caught and becoming slaves themselves. Most of the slave masters never survived for more than two weeks.

She must have told him to either release all his slaves or she would make sure that he got on that particular train.

I'll tell you now; if *Saturday night's alright for fighting* and I never had the Jets with me, then I would have no problems having Carla by my side and in my corner. She looks and sounds so sweet and peaceful but don't get her riled up. She can take care of herself."

"Rocket Man, I want to know what makes rotten peaches nectar turn into a calming kind of drink?" asked Nikita.

"It comes back down to the way in which the bacteria from the rotten peaches is extracted from the fruit and what it is mixed with. It can be mixed with anything and given properly; it can be used like the old time recreation drugs but without the bad side effects.

That's what I was giving Tiny to drink and why the water was cloudy. As you can see, it hasn't done her any harm.

I will never tell anyone how to extract the bacteria and I won't give it to anyone unless they want to try it." replied Robert

Tiny said "Look at me; *I'm still standing*. I actually enjoyed the taste of the nectar and I will drink it again if it is offered to me.

I am *blessed* that I was born with immunity against just about everything that your part of the Universe can offer. And now I even have immunity against the green mist; thanks to Daniel."

THE FINAL BROADCAST

Robert made all the arrangements to meet with his dad's friends at the *Country Comfort* Club on *Your Song* instead as he knew it would be quiet even for a Saturday night and it was one place that his dad used to regularly meet his friends the following night.

There was a time difference and Your Song was a day behind the Moon.

Once at the club, everybody knew where they had to be and St Peter informed the Enforcement Agency of their plan and would be waiting down on the corner to take the captives into official custody and jail.

Sitting at the table one of the men said "There's *something about the way you look tonight* that doesn't seem right. You seem to be a bit on edge about something and don't say you're not because it's been *sixty years on* since we first met and over the years I have grown to know your moods and your ways."

Just as Robert was about to answer him, the girls walked in on cue and sat at the table next to them and the men were distracted from their conversation and began listening to the girl's conversation.

Little Jeannie was saying *"I meant to do my work today* but Fred started again with his attempt to try to get me to go out with him. This time before we left the office he began with *"Can you feel the love tonight* because *I want love* from you?

Please *don't go breaking my heart* again by saying no to me. All I really want to know is; *are you ready for love* so that I can give you mine."

Carla replied "Well, you can only hope that he will find someone else if you keep rejecting him or find yourself someone and get married. You could invite him to your wedding and he can *kiss the bride* and then maybe he will get the message that you are not interested in him."

"Carla." said Little Jeannie "I am not interested in settling down yet; I still want to have fun and excitement.

I need you to turn to the time when Scarlet was still going out with us and then she met Hector; now look at her and how her life has changed.

She is like a *candle in the wind* that is ready to start an enormous fire with her mood swings."

Tiny glanced over to the guy's table and gave a quick smile to one of them before saying "*Love lies* many times but then all of a sudden you find the real thing comes along.

Stan told me once that he wanted to *take me to the pilot* and get married in space and then we would honeymoon in the Yellow Brick Road Mansion but I had heard some bad stuff about that place and said not on your life.

He said that the mansion that he was talking about was not the one on Earth but on Transvenus.

I asked him if he knew just how many Yellow Brick Road Houses, Motels, Hotels, Clubs, Mansions and actual Roads there were with that name scattered all over this universe.

His reply was a lot because it was a very popular name and sometimes it was good to say *goodbye Yellow Brick Road* whatever and other times it was not."

Medley, dressed as one of the waiters, approached the girl's table with a tray of drinks and a message that the gentlemen at the next table would like the girls to join them for the evening.

After the girls accepted the invitation and had joined the men, the conversation got back to where it had left off with Robert saying "I don't know what you mean. I am still the same person that you knew years ago Razor Face."

"When I said that there was *something about the way you look tonight* that was different; I wasn't wrong you are not the real Rocket Man.

Usually you take off your helmet so no-one knows who you are and just now you called me Razor Face and the real Rocket Man knows that Razor Face is locked up in jail on Earth and that I am his son.

Now take off your helmet and show your face." said Flat Top.

Stinker said as he reached down to the knife in his boot "No, he's not Rocket Man but an impostor and this is a trap." and went to grab Carla to take as a hostage.

Carla looked across the table at the other girls and said with excitement *"Someone saved my life tonight* as I was getting mighty frustrated and bored. You know it is true *Saturday's nights alright for fighting."* and she swung her fist at Stinker, hitting him in his left eye.

Little Jeannie and Tiny both reply *"Someone saved my life tonight* as well and I haven't had this much fun in years."

Before Robert or any of the other agents realized what was happening, the girls, after a short scuffle, had each of the criminals on the floor and begging *"Don't let the sun go down on me* in this club. It's bad enough having females taking us out and handing us over to the Enforcement Agency."

"Don't let the sun go down on me is something that you will have to ask the Enforcers at the place that they will

send you to. If they send you somewhere by train and the driver tells you that *this train don't stop there anymore;* then I would be mighty worried about your destination or if they put you on a special shuttle; you won't be able to asked anyone to *take me to the pilot* as your destination will be far away from any civilized planet." said Carla.

"I'm glad that *I'm still standing* because this *love song* that the *travellin' band* is playing is so beautiful and sad. *I guess that's why they call it the blues.* Now, *can I put you on* your final trip for today, Flat Top?

Yes, *someone saved my life tonight* too as it has been *sixty years on* since I last had so much enjoyment. I have come down in time and I have learned from these other two friends of mine that *if the river can bend,* then so can I and that people do accept you for *just the way you are.*" said Tiny

Robert looked at Tiny and said "*Someone saved my life tonight* too but not in the way that people would notice or think. *I want love* but *I don't mind* waiting for it as long it is the right kind of love and not a love that is a *candle in the wind* that can be snuffed out quickly.

Benny and the Jets, Captain Fantastic and the Brown Dirt Cowboys are all leaving now so I think that we had better join them and find out what we do next."

Tiny whispered in Robert's ear "*Are you ready for love* now because *I don't wanna go on with* you believing that you're not because of your father?

I have gotten to know you a bit and I *wouldn't have you any other way.*"

Everyone gathered outside the club and after the Enforcers had taken the criminals away, Mr. Brumby turned to St Peter and asked "*Where to now St Peter?*"

"Back to your office." was the reply "I have some explaining to do to everyone here. Please meet me there in three hours.

Oh and Frank, please tell them about your future plans for your agency before I get there."

Back at the office after some snacks, coffee and other drinks were served Mr. Brumby got everyone's attention and said "*Someone saved my life tonight* or should I say a large group of loyal employees did and I am so happy that *I'm still standing* to be able to talk to you all.

Many years ago I met someone and *she sold me magic* and it was from that magic that the *greatest discovery* so far has been made.

Thank you for a job well done.

Working as a team on such short notice proves that we all know our jobs and that is why I have decided to expand the company and semi retire.

Harry, I know how you like the office, so I have decided to train you to take over from me here.

Tom, you enjoy the more interesting side of the work and helping to make *the greatest discovery* to date so if you want to, I'll take you out to the lab and research place on Corona and train you to run that side of the agency.

Benny and the Jets is just a name for a well-oiled group of men; however Bennie, you will want to retire yourself sometime so I have decided to put you in charge of recruiting and training all our new agents along with Captain Fantastic. His group will carry on their name; that is if both of you would like to take the positions?

Carla would you please think it over and let me know if you would like to be in charge of a new office to be opened up on *Your Song*.

Now Tiny, I had originally thought that you might like to be in charge of a new office in *Levon* but seeing that you now have become close friends with Robert you may not wish to take the position.

Robert, now I know who you really are, I doubt that you would want to go back and live permanently in Crocodile Rock.

The Universal Enforcement Agency has asked me to set up an office just outside *Grey Seal* on the bad side of the moon and I was going to ask you if you would like the position.

Little Jeannie, I would like you and Nikita to become ambassadors for this agency. It will still mean travelling around the universe and sometimes having to asked crew members to *take me to the pilot* but there's *something about the way you look tonight* that I feel won't be difficult for either of you to handle.

Nikita, you have learned so much in the last few days that I would like you to go to Val Hala and study there for three months.

It has been nearly *sixty years on* from when I started training with my father and I would like to finally and completely retire in a couple of years and I have spent many hours thinking it over and talking to St Peter about it and both of us feel that everyone is completely competent to handle the new positions on offer. Now what do you say?"

Carla was the first to answer "I don't need to think it over; I would love to settle down on *Your song* as I would be living close to my family again.

I can't wait to get home to tell them.

I could also have my *Honky cat* with me. Thank you for considering me for the position."

Tiny said "If I take the position in *Levon* and Robert wants the position near Grey Seal; couldn't both places be managed on a part time basis.

If one of us got our license and a small shuttle then we would be able to get to both places without having to ask a crew member to *take me to the pilot*.

When I came here from my home planet I flew in a rented shuttle so I could easily convert my license to be able to fly all over this universe. I don't think that I would have much trouble converting it seeing as I am going to be a permanent employee and not a freelance agent for this agency anymore."

Mr. Brumby said "Now that is a good idea but Robert hasn't told us of his decision yet.

He may not want to settle in one place not yet; especially after what he has experienced and has learned during his time with this agency."

Robert replied "I think that you are both right. I have learned quite a bit and *I want love* but at the moment *I can't tell the bottom from the top*.

I know that *Saturday's night's alright for fighting* and *someone saved my life tonight* but I feel like the opened *tinderbox* that has the burning *candle in the wind* in it and I don't know if it is going to go out or not. I need some time to sort myself out."

Little Jeannie's answer was "I would love to be an Ambassador for the agency and I don't care how many times that I'll have to ask "*Take me to the pilot.*" because I just love travelling and meeting people.

It sure beats some of the undercover work that I had to do. *I guess that's why they call it the blues* once your assignment is finished and you have nothing to do. Now I won't have to worry about that and I can live a normal kind of life. Thank you Mr. Brumby for this opportunity."

Captain Fantastic's answer was "I agree with you about my retirement and I never have to say *take me to the pilot* because I am usually sitting in the cockpit with him.

Now if I accept your offer, are you going to pick my replacement or can I because I do have two people in mind that are both equally competent and will accept my decision and not cause any trouble for my replacement?

I need you to turn to when you had to select Jack Taylor's replacement and how that turned out. If your father hadn't stepped in at the last moment Jack wouldn't have lived for as long as he did.

Remember when Jack said that *she sold me magic* and that I had to *come and get it*. Your father had to take him to the empty garden to speak with Dixie Lily. Robert that's who you should go and see to get yourself sorted out."

Roy said "Dixie Lily used to be a dirty little street kid until she was given the chance to help others with her healing hands.

She really is a wonderful worker and a very good healer.

Frank when I leave here and go get Old 67; I think that I will also semi retire. I will still be available if I'm needed but like you I am getting a bit tired of traipsing around this universe and I would like to spend more time talking to my old soldier friends."

Bennie commented "Yes Robert, if you really want to get yourself sorted out then Dixie Lily would be right person to talk to. You would find that she would have a better understanding about what you've been through more than anyone else including St Peter.

Frank, I have been thinking it over and I feel the same as the Captain about my replacement because I would like to take up your offer for the new position. I have told my team many times *"Don't let the sun go down on me* while I'm out in the field."

I would like to spend more time at home now that I'm also getting on in years.

I know that my team will understand my decision and will support my replacement.

Someone saved my life tonight as well and I'm so grateful for that and Frank it was you and your offer that saved me."

Mr. Brumby replied "Thank you to all of you and Bennie and Captain you can select your own replacements.

Robert if you would like to spend some time with Dixie Lily then I'll arrange it for you. She has been very helpful to our agency in the past. It's time like these and what you are feeling; is why people say "*I guess that's why they call the blues* the blues. It will still be a matter of months before I need to know your final decision so take a bit of time to think about it.

Now Harry, Tom and Nikita I would like to know what your answers could be?"

"Well." said Tom "I think that working in the Lab and Research part would be very interesting and maybe we can still find a way to eliminate the green mist once and for all and also find an antidote for it in case someone else tries to copy the idea.

So yes dad, I would like to take your offer up."

Harry said "You know that you didn't have to ask me; I would have kept the office going no matter what. I found the books very interesting and I think that both Tom and I should keep them going for future generations. Shouldn't St Peter be here soon?"

"I don't know. Your offer sounds so tempting but *it's me that you need* to keep all the communications open, especially when our people are on..."

Nikita was interrupted and surprised when they all heard "*Rock me when he's gone.*" coming from the communications monitor that was supposed to be switched off.

They all rushed over and gathered around the monitor and saw the face of St Peter looking at them.

St Peter said "*Can you feel the love tonight* from the universe. There are a few things that I have to explain.

Nikita the night that you were affected by the green mist and you were reading the books; you did hear the night talking to you but it was Daniel and he was telling you about the offer that Mr. Brumby has given you but not in a direct way.

A replacement receptionist will be employed who will be very similar in her ways as you. She will be a great asset to the agency.

Mr. Brumby, many years ago the antidote was given to your agency but the young woman who gave it to you was really a *spirit in the sky*.

Tom you will be the one to work out the antidote for this green mist which unfortunately will still be around for about forty more years and then it will just disappear completely but your work will bring many more antidotes for many other illnesses and will also help solve many crimes.

Harry you will do a great job and your sons and grandsons will carry on the name for many years to come.

Robert, *I'm still standing* because of you and I thank you for that.

Your *original sin* is not the sin of your father, so go and see the girl in the empty garden for with her you will *recover your soul* and you will never have any more doubts about the rest of your life.

Little Jeannie, James said "*Don't go breaking my heart* and not take the offer because somewhere along the way you will meet your real man, who has *blue eyes* and you will marry him and have a very prosperous future in all ways."

Tiny, *whenever you're ready* to embark on your new life, Robert will be there beside you, but you must be careful if you decide to take him back to your planet because of the time difference.

You will want to take him back and when it is time we will protect him for a short while so that he can learn what your life growing up was like.

Your son will be just like his father; a good, gentle, caring man and will love listening and playing blues music.

He will be able to play in a very similar way as DBR does.

There is one other thing that you all should know; and that is you are *blessed* with the love that is *written in the stars* and you are always *in the hands of the angels* who will help you at any time.

They are not allowed to step in and take control over a situation; however when asked they can direct and guide you to the right path, just like they have done in the past that has meant that the green mist issue has been solved.

They knew what Robert's father was doing but were not allowed to stop him so they started giving clues and guiding you all to meet the right people to help you long the way. With the angels by your side you may never have to *recover your soul* unless you change into a criminal.

Daniel has been around for many years helping people especially this agency and your relatives. In the beginning he was known as Earth Angel David but when the move to outer space started happening, he changed his name to Daniel and enlisted the aid of many of his friends like James, Dan Dare and me.

We all have *blue eyes* that are unforgettable and we are all just a *spirit in the sky* that will come to you or anybody when we are needed.

Now it is time for me to *return to paradise* in the *Tower of Babel* for some well-earned rest. *Someone saved my life tonight* again and now I am back *signed sealed delivered* to my maker.

St Peter's face disappeared from the screen and it was replaced by Madonna's face and she was saying to someone on her right "You're trying to tell me that it was *something about the way you look tonight* and *someone saved my life tonight* because there's *no shoe strings on Louise*'s shoes.

Are you crazy?" then she turned and looked into the monitor and made a startled Oh! "Mr. Brumby, have you heard that the extension to the Karmatron mission had been finished and it has been dedicated to St Peter who passed away two years ago after a long illness that kept him bound to the mission for almost ten years."

Everyone who was standing around the monitor, just looked at each other in disbelief then Mr. Brumby said "I had a feeling years ago that we were being helped but I never knew who was helping. Keeping my faith and doing what I believed was right for everyone has paid off.

Sometimes I used to ask myself "Was I doing things right and who would help me if I needed help and now my questions have been answered."

A voice came through the speakers "Keep your faith and believe in yourselves that you can do whatever you what to do or become whoever you want to be. If you need help just ask and we will help you although it may not be in the way that you think of but we will help and will keep watch over you all."

Then there was nothing but a blank monitor screen and silence in the room.

REFERENCE

GOODBYE YELLOW BRICK ROAD CD
FUNERAL FOR A FRIEND (LOVE LIES BLEEDING)
CANDLE IN THE WIND
BENNIE AND THE JETS
GOODBYE YELLOW BRICK ROAD
THIS SONG HAS NO TITLE
GREY SEAL
JAMAICA JERK OFF
I'VE SEEN THAT MOVIE TOO
SWEET PAINTED LADY
BALLAD OF DANNY BAILEY, THE (1909-1934)
DIRTY LITTLE GIRL
ALL THE GIRLS LOVE ALICE
YOUR SISTER CAN'T TWIST (BUT SHE CAN ROCK 'N ROLL)
SATURDAY NIGHT'S ALRIGHT FOR FIGHTING
ROY ROGERS
SOCIAL DISEASE
HARMONY

LOVE SONGS CD

CAN YOU FEEL THE LOVE TONIGHT?
ONE
SACRIFICE
DANIEL
SOMEONE SAVED MY LIFE TONIGHT
YOUR SONG
DON'T LET THE SUN GO DOWN ON ME
(WITH GEORGE MICHAEL, GEORGE
MICHAEL)
BELIEVE
BLUE EYES
SORRY SEEMS TO BE THE HARDEST
WORD
BLESSED
CANDLE IN THE WIND
YOU CAN MAKE HISTORY (YOUNG
AGAIN)
NO VALENTINES
CIRCLE OF LIFE

ELTON JOHN CD

YOUR SONG
I NEED YOU TO TURN TO
TAKE ME TO THE PILOT
NO SHOE STRINGS ON LOUISE

FIRST EPISODE AT HIENTON
SIXTY YEARS ON
BORDER SONG
GREATEST DISCOVERY
CAGE
KING MUST DIE
BAD SIDE OF THE MOON
GREY SEAL
ROCK AND ROLL MADONNA

UNION CD
IF IT WASN'T FOR BAD
EIGHT HUNDRED DOLLAR SHOES
HEY AHAB
GONE TO SHILOH
HEARTS HAVE TURNED TO STONE
JIMMIE RODGERS' DREAM
THERE'S NO TOMORROW
MONKEY SUIT
BEST PART OF THE DAY
DREAM COME TRUE
I SHOULD HAVE SENT ROSES
WHEN LOVE IS DYING
MY KIND OF HELL
MANDALAY AGAIN
NEVER TOO OLD (TO HOLD SOMEBODY)

IN THE HANDS OF ANGELS

**GREATEST HITS DEFINITIVE ALBUM
1970-2002 CD
DISC 1**
YOUR SONG
LEVON
TINY DANCER
ROCKET MAN (IT'S GOING TO BE LONG,
LONG TIME)
HONKY CAT
CROCODILE ROCK
DANIEL
SATURDAY'S NIGHT'S ALRIGHT (FOR
FIGHTING)
GOODBYE YELLOW BRICK ROAD
CANDLE IN THE WIND
BENNIE AND THE JETS
DON'T LET THE SUN GO DOWN ON ME
BITCH IS BACK
PHILADELPHIA FREEDOM
SOMEONE SAVED MY LIFE TONIGHT
ISLAND GIRL
SORRY SEEMS TO BE THE HARDEST
WORD

DISC 2

DON'T GO BREAKING MY HEART (WITH
KIKI DEE, KIKI DEE)
LITTLE JEANNIE
I'M STILL STANDING
I GUESS THAT'S WHY THEY CALL IT
THE BLUES
SAD SONGS (SAY SO MUCH)
I DON'T WANNA GO ON WITH YOU
LIKE THAT
NIKITA
SACRIFICE
ONE
CAN YOU FEEL THE LOVE TONIGHT
CIRCLE OF LIFE
BELIEVE
BLESSED
SOMETHING ABOUT THE WAY YOU
LOOK TONIGHT
WRITTEN IN THE STARS (WITH LEANN
RIMES, LEANN RIMES)
I WANT LOVE
THIS TRAIN DON'T STOP THERE
ANYMORE

GREATEST HITS CD
YOUR SONG
DANIEL
HONKY CAT
GOODBYE YELLOW BRICK ROAD
SATURDAY NIGHT'S ALRIGHT FOR
FIGHTING
ROCKET MAN (I THINK IT'S GOING TO
BE A LONG, LONG TIME)
BENNIE AND THE JETS
CANDLE IN THE WIND
DON'T LET THE SUN GO DOWN ON ME
BORDER SONG
CROCODILE ROCK

CAPTAIN FANTASTIC AND THE BROWN DIRT COWBOY CD
CAPTAIN FANTASTIC AND THE BROWN
DIRT COWBOY
TOWER OF BABEL
BITTER FINGERS
TELL ME WHEN THE WHISTLE BLOWS
SOMEONE SAVED MY LIFE TONIGHT
(GOTTA GET A) MEAL TICKET
BETTER OFF DEAD
WRITING

WE ALL FALL IN LOVE SOMETIMES
CURTAINS
LUCY IN THE SKY WITH DIAMONDS
ONE DAY (AT A TIME)
PHILADELPHIA FREEDOM

TUMBLEWEED CONNECTION CD
DISC 1
BALLAD OF A WELL-KNOWN GUN
COME DOWN IN TIME
COUNTRY COMFORT
SON OF YOUR FATHER
MY FATHER'S GUN
WHERE TO NOW ST. PETER?
LOVE SONG
AMOREENA
TALKING OLD SOLDIERS
BURN DOWN THE MISSION
INTO THE OLD MAN'S SHOES
MADMAN ACROSS THE WATER
DISC 2
THERE GOES A WELL KNOWN GUN
COME DOWN IN TIME
COUNTRY COMFORT
SON OF YOUR FATHER
TALKING OLD SOLDIERS

INTO THE OLD MAN'S SHOES
SISTERS OF THE CROSS
MADMAN ACROSS THE WATER
INTO THE OLD MAN'S SHOES
MY FATHER'S GUN (BBC SESSION)
BALLAD OF A WELL-KNOWN GUN (BBC SESSION)
BURN DOWN THE MISSION (BBC SESSION) (DIFFERENT VERSION)
AMOREENA (BBC SESSION)

ROCKET MAN: THE DEFINITIVE HITS CD - IMPORT

BENNIE & THE JETS
PHILADELPHIA FREEDOM
DANIEL
ROCKET MAN (I THINK IT'S GOING TO BE A LONG LONG TIME)
I GUESS THAT'S WHY THEY CALL IT THE BLUES
TINY DANCER
DON'T LET THE SUN GO DOWN ON ME
I WANT LOVE
CANDLE IN THE WIND
BITCH IS BACK
I'M STILL STANDING

SATURDAY NIGHT'S ALRIGHT (FOR FIGHTING)
YOUR SONG
SORRY SEEMS TO BE THE HARDEST WORD
CAN YOU FEEL THE LOVE TONIGHT
GOODBYE YELLOW BRICK ROAD
TINDERBOX
ARE YOU READY FOR LOVE
BENNIE & THE JETS
ROCKET MAN
CANDLE IN THE WIND
SATURDAY NIGHT'S ALRIGHT (FOR FIGHTING)
YOUR SONG
YOUR SONG (ELTON IN FOUR DECADES VIDEO)
I GUESS THAT'S WHY THEY CALL IT THE BLUES (ELTON IN FOUR DECADES VIDEO)
I'M STILL STANDING (ELTON IN FOUR DECADES VIDEO)
I WANT LOVE (ELTON IN FOUR DECADES VIDEO)
TINDERBOX (VIDEO)

TOO LOW FOR ZERO CD
COLD AS CHRISTMAS (IN THE MIDDLE OF THE YEAR)
I'M STILL STANDING
TOO LOW FOR ZERO
RELIGION
I GUESS THAT'S WHY THEY CALL IT THE BLUES
CRYSTAL
KISS THE BRIDE
WHIPPING BOY
SAINT
ONE MORE ARROW
EARN WHILE YOU LEARN LORD CHOC ICE
DREAMBOAT
RETREAT

GREATEST HITS 1970-2002 CD
DISC 1
YOUR SONG
LEVON
TINY DANCER
ROCKET MAN (IT'S GOING TO BE LONG, LONG TIME)
HONKY CAT

CROCODILE ROCK
DANIEL
SATURDAY'S NIGHT'S ALRIGHT (FOR FIGHTING)
GOODBYE YELLOW BRICK ROAD
CANDLE IN THE WIND
BENNIE AND THE JETS
DON'T LET THE SUN GO DOWN ON ME
BITCH IS BACK
PHILADELPHIA FREEDOM
SOMEONE SAVED MY LIFE TONIGHT
ISLAND GIRL
SORRY SEEMS TO BE THE HARDEST WORD

DISC 2
DON'T GO BREAKING MY HEART (WITH KIKI DEE, KIKI DEE)
LITTLE JEANNIE
I'M STILL STANDING
I GUESS THAT'S WHY THEY CALL IT THE BLUES
SAD SONGS (SAY SO MUCH)
I DON'T WANNA GO ON WITH YOU LIKE THAT
NIKITA
SACRIFICE

ONE
CAN YOU FEEL THE LOVE TONIGHT
CIRCLE OF LIFE
BELIEVE
BLESSED
SOMETHING ABOUT THE WAY YOU
LOOK TONIGHT
WRITTEN IN THE STARS (WITH LEANN
RIMES, LEANN RIMES)
I WANT LOVE
THIS TRAIN DON'T STOP THERE
ANYMORE

MADMAN ACROSS THE WATER CD
TINY DANCER
LEVON
RAZOR FACE
MADMAN ACROSS THE WATER
INDIAN SUNSET
HOLIDAY INN
ROTTEN PEACHES
ALL THE NASTIES
GOODBYE

CARIBOU CD
BITCH IS BACK
PINKY

GRIMSBY
DIXIE LILY
SOLAR PRESTIGE A GAMMON
YOU'RE SO STATIC
I'VE SEEN THE SAUCERS
STINKER
DON'T LET THE SUN GO DOWN ON ME
TICKING
PINBALL WIZARD
SICK CITY
COLD HIGHWAY
STEP INTO CHRISTMAS

ELTON JOHN - 11-17-70 CD
BAD SIDE OF THE MOON
AMOREENA
TAKE ME TO THE PILOT
SIXTY YEARS ON
HONKY TONK WOMEN
CAN I PUT YOU ON
BURN DOWN THE MISSION INCLUDING /
MY BABY LEFT ME / GET BACK

LIVE IN AUSTRALIA CD
SIXTY YEARS ON
I NEED YOU TO TURN TO
GREATEST DISCOVERY

TONIGHT
SORRY SEEMS TO BE THE HARDEST
WORD
KING MUST DIE
TAKE ME TO THE PILOT
TINY DANCER
HAVE MERCY ON THE CRIMINAL
MADMAN ACROSS THE WATER
CANDLE IN THE WIND
BURN DOWN THE MISSION
YOUR SONG
DON'T LET THE SUN GO DOWN ON ME

**TWO ROOMS: CELEBRATING THE
SONGS OF ELTON JOHN & BERNIE
TAUPIN. CD ELTON JOHN / BERNIE
TAUPIN TRIBUTE TO JOHN, ELTON /
TAUPIN, BERNIE**
BORDER SONG
ROCKET MAN (I THINK IT'S GOING TO
BE A LONG, LONG TIME)
COME DOWN IN TIME
SATURDAY NIGHT'S ALRIGHT FOR
FIGHTING
CROCODILE ROCK
DANIEL

SORRY SEEMS TO BE THE HARDEST
WORD
LEVON
BITCH IS BACK
PHILADELPHIA FREEDOM
YOUR SONG
DON'T LET THE SUN GO DOWN ON ME
MADMAN ACROSS THE WATER
SACRIFICE
BURN DOWN THE MISSION
TONIGHT

FOX CD
BREAKING DOWN THE BARRIERS
HEART IN THE RIGHT PLACE
JUST LIKE BELGIUM
NOBODY WINS
FASCIST FACES
CARLA/ETUDE/FANFARE/CHLOE
HEELS OF THE WIND
ELTON'S SONG
FOX

**DON'T SHOOT ME I'M ONLY THE
PIANO PLAYER CD**
DANIEL
TEACHER I NEED YOU

ELDERBERRY WINE
BLUES FOR MY BABY AND ME
MIDNIGHT CREEPER
HAVE MERCY ON THE CRIMINAL
I'M GOING TO BE A TEENAGE IDOL
TEXAN LOVE SONG
CROCODILE ROCK
HIGH FLYING BIRD
SCREW YOU (YOUNG MAN'S BLUES)
JACK RABBIT
WHENEVER YOU'RE READY (WE'LL GO
STEADY AGAIN)
SKYLINE PIGEON

HONKY CHATEAU CD
HONKY CAT
MELLOW
I THINK I'M GOING TO KILL MYSELF
SUSIE (DRAMAS)
ROCKET MAN (I THINK IT'S GOING TO
BE A LONG, LONG TIME)
SALVATION
SLAVE
AMY
MONA LISAS AND MAD HATTERS
HERCULES

SLAVE

SINGLE MAN CD
SHINE THROUGH
RETURN TO PARADISE
I DON'T CARE
BIG DIPPER
IT AIN'T GONNA BE EASY
PART-TIME LOVE
GEORGIA
SHOOTING STAR
MADNESS
REVERIE
SONG FOR GUY
EGO
FLINSTONE BOY
I CRY AT NIGHT
LOVESICK
STRANGERS

**COMPLETE THOM BELL SESSIONS
CD**
NICE AND SLOW
COUNTRY LOVE SONG
SHINE ON THROUGH
MAMA CAN'T BUY YOU LOVE
ARE YOU READY FOR LOVE

THREE WAY LOVE AFFAIR

SLEEPING WITH THE PAST CD
DURBAN DEEP
HEALING HANDS
WHISPERS
CLUB AT THE END OF THE STREET
SLEEPING WITH THE PAST
STONE'S THROW FROM HURTIN'
SACRIFICE
I NEVER KNEW HER NAME
AMAZES ME
BLUE AVENUE
DANCING IN THE END ZONE
LOVE IS A CANNIBAL

JUMP UP CD
DEAR JOHN
SPITEFUL CHILD
BALL & CHAIN
LEGAL BOYS
I AM YOUR ROBOT
BLUE EYES
EMPTY GARDEN (HEY HEY JOHNNY)
PRINCESS
WHERE HAVE ALL THE GOOD TIMES
GONE?

ALL QUIET ON THE WESTERN FRONT

ICE ON FIRE CD
THIS TOWN
CRY TO HEAVEN
SOUL GLOVE
NIKITA
TOO YOUNG
WRAP HER UP GEORGE MICHAEL,
GEORGE MICHAEL ELTON JOHN
SATELLITE
TELL ME WHAT THE PAPERS SAY
CANDY BY THE POUND
SHOOT DOWN THE MOON
MAN WHO NEVER DIED
RESTLESS
SORRY SEEMS TO BE THE HARDEST
WORD
I'M STILL STANDING JEAN-YVES
LIEVAUX, JEAN-YVES LIEVAUX ELTON
JOHN

REG STRIKES BACK CD
TOWN OF PLENTY
WORD IN SPANISH
MONA LISAS AND MAD HATTERS, PT. 2
JAPANESE HANDS

I DON'T WANNA GO ON WITH YOU
LIKE THAT
GOODBYE MARLON BRANDO
CAMERA NEVER LIES
HEAVY TRAFFIC
POOR COW
SINCE GOD INVENTED GIRLS
ROPE AROUND A FOOL
I DON'T WANNA GO ON WITH YOU
LIKE THAT
I DON'T WANNA GO ON WITH YOU
LIKE THAT
MONA LISAS AND MAD HATTERS, PT.2

REG STRIKES BACK CD (3 DISC)
DISC 1
FUNERAL FOR A FRIEND/LOVE LIES
BLEEDING
SATURDAY NIGHT'S ALRIGHT (FOR
FIGHTING)
BURN DOWN THE MISSION
GOODBYE YELLOW BRICK ROAD
I GUESS THAT'S WHY THEY CALL IT THE
BLUES
DANIEL
HONKY CAT

I WANT LOVE
ROCKET MAN
SAD SONGS (SAY SO MUCH)
TAKE ME TO THE PILOT
SORRY
TINY DANCER
(SACRIFICE)
DON'T LET THE SUN GO DOWN ON ME
ALL THE YOUNG GIRLS LOVE ALICE
CANDLE IN THE WIND
SKYLINE PIGEON
ARE YOU READY FOR LOVE
BENNIE
BITCH IS BACK
CROCODILE ROCK
I'M STILL STANDING
YOUR SONG
DISC 2
SORRY SEEMS TO BE THE HARDEST
WORD
BENNIE AND THE JETS
BENNIE AND THE JETS
DISC 3
(CD-ROM TRACK) NOT USED IN STORY

MADE IN ENGLAND CD
BELIEVE
MADE IN ENGLAND
HOUSE
COLD
PAIN
BELFAST
LATITUDE
PLEASE
MAN
LIES
BLESSED

ROCK OF THE WESTIES CD
MEDLEY: YELL HELP/WEDNESDAY
NIGHT/UGLY: YELL HELP / WEDNESDAY
NIGHT / UGLY
DAN DARE (PILOT OF THE FUTURE)
ISLAND GIRL
GROW SOME FUNK OF YOUR OWN
I FEEL LIKE A BULLET (IN THE GUN OF
ROBERT FORD)
STREET KIDS
HARD LUCK STORY
FEED ME
BILLY BONES AND THE WHITE BIRD

PLANES
SUGAR ON THE FLOOR

CAPTAIN & THE KID CD
POSTCARDS FROM RICHARD NIXON
JUST LIKE NOAH'S ARK
WOULDN'T HAVE IT ANY OTHER WAY
(NYC)
TINDERBOX
AND THE HOUSE FELL DOWN
BLUES NEVER FADE AWAY
BRIDGE
I MUST HAVE LOST IT ON THE WIND
OLD 67
CAPTAIN & THE KID

GREATEST HITS 1976-1986 CD
I'M STILL STANDING
MAMA CAN'T BUY YOU LOVE
SORRY SEEMS TO BE THE HARDEST
WORD
LITTLE JEANNIE
BLUE EYES
DON'T GO BREAKING MY HEART (WITH
KIKI DEE, KIKI DEE)
EMPTY GARDEN (HEY, HEY JOHNNY)
KISS THE BRIDE

I GUESS THAT'S WHY THEY CALL IT
THE BLUES
WHO WEARS THESE SHOES?
SAD SONGS (SAY SO MUCH)
WRAP HER UP GEORGE MICHAEL,
GEORGE MICHAEL ELTON JOHN
NIKITA

VICTIM OF LOVE CD
JOHNNY B GOODE
WARM LOVE IN A COLD WORLD
BORN BAD
THUNDER IN THE NIGHT
SPOTLIGHT
STREET BOOGIE
VICTIM OF LOVE

**PEACHTREE ROAD: SPECIAL
COLLECTOR'S EDITION CD**
WEIGHT OF THE WORLD
PORCH SWING IN TUPELO
ANSWER IN THE SKY
TURN THE LIGHTS OUT WHEN YOU
LEAVE
MY ELUSIVE DRUG
THEY CALL HER THE CAT
FREAKS IN LOVE

ALL THAT I'M ALLOWED
I STOP AND I BREATHE
TOO MANY TEARS
IT'S GETTING DARK IN HERE
I CAN'T KEEP THIS FROM YOU
LETTER
MERRY CHRISTMAS MAGGIE THATCHER

**GREATEST HITS/ONE NIGHT ONLY
DELUXE SOUND & VISION
(DVD/PAL-0) CD**
YOUR SONG
TINY DANCER
HONKY CAT
ROCKET MAN (I THINK IT'S GOING TO
BE A LONG LONG TIME)
CROCODILE ROCK
DANIEL
SATURDAY NIGHT'S ALRIGHT FOR
FIGHTING
OODBYE YELOW BRICK ROAD
CANDLE IN THE WIND
BENNIE & THE JETS
DON'T LET THE SUN GO DOWN ON ME
BITCH IS BACK
PHILADELPHIA FREEDOM

SOMEONE SAVED MY LIFE TONIGHT
ISLAND GIRL
DON'T GO BREAKING MY HEART (WITH
KIKI DEE)
SORRY SEEMS TO E THE HARDEST
WORD
BLUE EYES
I'M STILL STANDING
I GUESS THAT'S WHY THEY CALL IT
THE BLUES
SAD SONGS (SAY SO MUCH)
NIKITA
SACRIFICE
ONE
KISS THE BRIDE
CAN YOU FEEL THE LOVE TONIGHT
CIRCLE OF LIFE
BELIEVE
MADE IN ENGLAND
SOMETHING ABOUT THE WAY YOU
LOOK TONIGHT
WRITTEN IN THE STARS (WITH LEANN
RIMES)
I WANT LOVE
THIS TRAIN DON'T STOP THERE
ANYMORE

SONG FOR GUY

FUNERAL FOR A FRIEND (LOVE LIES BLEEDING) (DVD)

CANDLE IN THE WIND (DVD)

BENNIE & THE JETS (DVD)

GOODBYE YELLOW BRICK ROAD (FT BILLY JOEL) (DVD)

SOMEONE SAVED MY LIFE TONIGHT (DVD)

LITTLE JEANNIE (DVD)

PHILADELPHIA FREEDOM (DVD)

TINY DANCER (DVD)

CAN YOU FEEL THE LOVE TONIGHT (DVD)

DANIEL (DVD)

ROCKET MAN (DVD)

CLUB AT THE END OF THE STREET (DVD)

BLUE EYES (DVD)

I GUESS THAT'S WHY THEY CALL IT THE BLUES (FT MARY J BLIGE) (DVD)

ONE (DVD)

I DON'T WANNA GO OUT LIKE THAT (DVD)

SORRY SEEM TO BE THE HARDEST WORD (DVD)

SACRIFICE (DVD)
COME TOGETHER (DVD)
YOUR SONG (FT RONAN KEATING)
(DVD)
SAD SONG (SAY SO MUCH) (FT BRYAN
ADAMS) (DVD)
I'M STILL STANDING (DVD)
CROCODILE ROCK (DVD)
SATURDAY NIGHT'S ALRIGHT OR
FIGHTING (FT ANASTACIA) (DVD)
BITCH IS BACK (DVD)
DON'T LET THE SUN GO DOWN ON ME
(DVD)
DON'T GO BREAKING MY HEART (FT
KIKI DEE) (DVD)
I WANT LOVE (VIDEO FT ROBERT
DOWNEY JR.)
THIS TRAIN DON'T STOP THERE
ANYMORE (VIDEO FT JUSTIN
TIMBERLAKE)
ORIGINAL SIN (VIDEO FT MANDY
MOORE & ELIZABETH TAYLOR)
SORRY SEEMS TO BE THE HARDEST
WORD (VIDEO FT BLUE)
ORIGINAL SIN

TWO ROOMS-CELEBRATING DVD
LOGOS
SATURDAY NIGHT'S ALRIGHT (FOR
FIGHTING)
SKYLINE PIGEON
BORDER SONG
BURN DOWN THE MISSION
TINY DANCER
SACRIFICE
DANIEL
YOUR SONG
COME DOWN IN TIME
SOMEONE SAVED MY LIFE TONIGHT
INTERVIEW / DODGERS STADIUM
(NOT USED IN STORY)
PHILADELPHIA FREEDOM
SORRY SEEMS TO BE THE HARDEST
WORD
TONGITH
EMPTY GARDEN
BENNIE AND THE JETS
BITCH IS BACK
CANDLE IN THE WIND
CREDITS

INSTRUMENTAL MEMORIES CD - IMPORT

ROCKET MAN INSTRUMENTAL MEMORIES
GOODBYE YELLOW BRICK ROAD INSTRUMENTAL MEMORIES
BLUE EYES INSTRUMENTAL MEMORIES
NIKITA INSTRUMENTAL MEMORIES
DONT GO BREAKING MY HEART INSTRUMENTAL MEMORIES
SACRIFICE INSTRUMENTAL MEMORIES
DANIEL INSTRUMENTAL MEMORIES
SONG FOR GUY INSTRUMENTAL MEMORIES
CROCODILE ROCK INSTRUMENTAL MEMORIES
SAD SONGS INSTRUMENTAL MEMORIES
CAN YOU FEEL THE LOVE TONIGHT INSTRUMENTAL MEMORIES
BENNY AND THE JETS INSTRUMENTAL MEMORIES
YOUR SONG INSTRUMENTAL MEMORIES
I GUESS THATS WHY THEY CALL IT THE BLUES INSTRUMENTAL MEMORIES
CANDLE IN THE WIND INSTRUMENTAL MEMORIES

DONT LET THE SUN GO DOWN ON ME
INSTRUMENTAL MEMORIES

**LEGENDARY COVERS AS SUNG BY
ELTON JOHN CD**
COTTONFIELDS
LADY D'ARBANVILLE
NATURAL SINNER
SPIRIT IN THE SKY
TRAVELIN' BAND
I CAN'T TELL THE BOTTOM FROM
THE TOP
GOOD MORNING FREEDOM
YOUNG, GIFTED, AND BLACK
IN THE SUMMERTIME
UP AROUND THE BEND
SHE SOLD ME MAGIC
COME AND GET IT
LOVE OF THE COMMON PEOPLE
SIGNED SEALED DELIVEREDD
IT'S ALL IN THE GAME
YELLOW RIVER

GREATEST HITS VOL. 3 CD
BITCH IS BACK
LUCY IN THE SKY WITH DIAMONDS
TINY DANCER

I FEEL LIKE A BULLET (IN THE GUN
OF ROBERT FORD)
SOMEONE SAVED MY LIFE TONIGHT
PHILADELPHIA FREEDOM
ISLAND GIRL
GROW SOME FUNK OF YOUR OWN
LEVON
PINBALL WIZARD

DUETS CD
TEARDROPS
WHEN I THINK ABOUT LOVE
POWER
SHAKEY GROUND
TRUE LOVE
IF YOU WERE ME
WOMAN'S NEEDS
OLD FRIEND
GO ON AND ON
DON'T GO BREAKING MY HEART
AIN'T NOTHING LIKE THE REAL THING
I'M YOUR PUPPET
LOVE LETTERS
BORN TO LOSE
DON'T LET THE SUN GO DOWN ON ME
DUETS FOR ONE

HERE & THERE CD - IMPORT
SKYLINE PIGEON
BORDER SONG
HONKY CAT
LOVE SONG
CROCIDILE ROCK
FUNERAL FOR A FRIEND
ROCKET MAN
BENNIE AND THE JETS
TAKE ME TO THE PILOT

RED PIANO TOUR CD
BENNIE
PHILADELPHIA FREEDOM
BELIEVE
DANIEL
ROCKET MAN
BLUES
SOMEONE SAVED MY LIFE TONIGHT
GOODBYE YELLOW BRICK ROAD
NIKITA
TINY DANCER
DON'T LET THE SUN
SORRY
CANDLE IN THE WIND
PINBALL WIZARD

BITCH IS BACK
I'M STILL STANDING
SATURDAY NIGHTS ALRIGHT
YOUR SONG

KARAOKE: ELTON JOHN CD
ROCKET MAN (GUIDE VOCALS)
YOUR SONG (EB)
CROCODILE ROCK
BENNIE AND THE JETS (GUIDE VOCALS)
GOODBYE YELLOW BRICK ROAD (F)
SORRY SEEMS TO BE THE HARDEST
WORD (GUIDE VOCALS)
ROCKET MAN (PERFORMANCE TRACK)
YOUR SONG (PERFORMANCE TRACK)
CROCODILE ROCK
BENNIE AND THE JETS (G)
GOODBYE YELLOW BRICK ROAD
(PERFORMANCE TRACK)
SORRY SEEMS TO BE THE HARDEST
WORD (PERFORMANCE TRACK)

GOODBYE YELLOW BRICK ROAD (MINI LP SLEEVE) CD
FUNERAL FOR A FRIEND/LOVE LIES
BLEEDING
CANDLE IN THE WIND

BENNIE AND THE JETS
GOODBYE YELLOW BRICK ROAD
THIS SONG HAS NO TITLE
GREY SEAL
JAMAICA JERK-OFF
I'VE SEEN THAT MOVIE TOO
SWEET PAINTED LADY
BALLAD OF DANNY BAILEY (1909-34)
DIRTY LITTLE GIRL
ALL THE GIRLS LOVE ALICE
YOUR SISTER CAN'T TWIST (BUT SHE
CAN ROCK & ROLL)
SATURDAY NIGHT'S ALRIGHT FOR
FIGHTING
ROY ROGERS
SOCIAL DISEASE
HARMONY

SONGS FROM THE WEST COAST CD
EMPEROR'S NEW CLOTHES
DARK DIAMOND
LOOK MA, NO HANDS
AMERICAN TRIANGLE
ORIGINAL SIN
BIRDS
I WANT LOVE

WASTELAND
BALLAD OF THE BOY IN THE RED SHOES
LOVE HER LIKE ME
MANSFIELD
THIS TRAIN DON'T STOP THERE
ANYMORE

VERY BEST OF ELTON JOHN CD
YOUR SONG
ROCKET MAN (I THINK IT'S
HONKY CAT
CROCODILE ROCK
DANIEL
GOODBYE YELLOW BRICK ROAD
SATURDAY NIGHT'S ALRIGHT
CANDLE IN THE WIND
DONT LET THE SUN GO DOWN
LUCY IN THE SKY WITH DIAM
PHILADELPHIA FREEDOM
SOMEONE SAVED MY LIFE TON
PINBALL WIZARD
BITCH IS BACK
DONT GO BREAKING MY HEART
BENNIE AND THE JETS
SORRY SEEMS TO BE THE HAR
PART TIME LOVE

BLUE EYES
I GUESS THATS WHY THEY CA
IM STILL STANDING
KISS THE BRIDE
SAD SONGS (SAY SO MUCH)
PASSENGERS
NIKITA
I DON'T WANNA GO ON WITH
SACRIFICE
EASIER TO WALK AWAY
YOU GOTTA LOVE SOMEONE

**TO BE CONTINUED... CD
DISC 1**
COME BACK BABY
LADY SAMANTHA
IT'S ME THAT YOU NEED
YOUR SONG
ROCK AND ROLL MADONNA
BAD SIDE OF THE MOON
YOUR SONG
TAKE ME TO THE PILOT
BORDER SONG
SIXTY YEARS ON
COUNTRY COMFORT
GRAY SEAL

FRIENDS
LEVON
TINY DANCER
MADMAN ACROSS THE WATER
HONKY CAT
MONA LISA AND MAD HATTERS
DISC 2
ROCKET MAN
DANIEL
CROCODILE ROCK
BENNIE AND THE JETS
GOODBYE YELLOW BRICK ROAD
ALL THE GIRLS LOVE ALICE
FUNERAL FOR A FRIEND / LOVE LIES
BLEEDING
WHENEVER YOU'RE READY (WE'LL GO
STEADY)
SATURDAY NIGHT'S ALRIGHT FOR
FIGHTING
JACK RABBIT
HARMONY
YOUNG MAN'S BLUES
STEP INTO CHRISTMAS
BITCH IS BACK
PINBALL WIZARD
SOMEONE SAVED MY LIFE TONIGHT

DISC 3

PHILADELPHIA FREEDOM
ONE DAY AT A TIME
LUCY IN THE SKY WITH DIAMONDS
I SAW HER STANDING THERE LIVE
W/JOHN LENNON
ISLAND GIRL
SORRY SEEMS TO BE THE HARDEST
WORD
DON'T GO BREAKING MY HEART
I FEEL LIKE A BULLET (IN THE GUN OF
ROBERT FORD)
EGO
SONG FOR GUY
MAMA CAN'T BUY YOU LOVE
CARTIER
LITTLE JEANNIE
DONNER POUR DONNER FRANCE GALL,
FRANCE GALL ELTON JOHN
FANFARE / CHLOE
RETREAT
BLUE EYES

DISC 4

EMPTY GARDEN (HEY HEY JOHNNY)
I GUESS THAT'S WHY THEY CALL IT
THE BLUES

I'M STILL STANDING
SAD SONGS (SAY SO MUCH)
ACT OF WAR MILLIE JACKSON, MILLIE
JACKSON ELTON JOHN
NIKITA
CANDLE IN THE WIND
CARLA ETUDE
DON'T LET THE SUN GO DOWN ON ME
I DON'T WANT TO GO ON WITH YOU
LIKE THAT
GIVE PEACE A CHANCE
SACRIFICE
MADE FOR ME
YOU GOTTA LOVE SOMEONE
I SWEAR I HEARD THE NIGHT TALKIN'
EASIER TO WALK AWAY

THE ONE CD
SIMPLE LIFE
ONE
SWEAT IT OUT
RUNAWAY TRAIN
WHITEWASH COUNTY
NORTH
WHEN A WOMAN DOESN'T WANT YOU
EMILY

ON DARK STREET
UNDERSTANDING WOMEN
LAST SONG

16 LEGENDARY COVERS FROM 1969-70 CD

I'M A NATURAL SINNER
UNITED WE STAND
SPIRIT IN THE SKY
TRAVELIN' BAND
TO BE YOUNG GIFTED AND BLACK
GOOD MORNING FREEDOM
UP AROUND THE BEND
IN THE SUMMERTIME
COME AND GET IT
LOVE OF THE COMMON PEOPLE
NEANDERTHAL MAN
I CAN'T TELL THE BOTTOM FROM
THE TOP
YELLOW RIVER
MY BABY LOVES LOVIN'
COTTON FIELDS
LADY D'ARBANVILLE

LADY SAMANTHA CD

ROCK AND ROLL MADONNA
WHENEVER YOURE READY

BAD SIDE OF THE MOON
JACK RABBIT
INTO THE OLD MANS SHOES
ITS ME THAT YOU NEED
HO HO HO
SKYLINE PIGEON
SCREW YOU
JUST LIKE STRANGE RAIN
GREY SEAL
HONEY ROLL
LADY SAMANTHA
FRIENDS

LEATHER JACKETS CD
LEATHER JACKETS
HOOP OF FIRE
DON'T TRUST THAT WOMAN
GO IT ALONE
GYPSY HEART
SLOW RIVERS CLIFF RICHARD, CLIFF
RICHARD ELTON JOHN
HEARTACHE ALL OVER THE WORLD
ANGELINE
MEMORY OF LOVE
PARIS
I FALL APART

CHARTBUSTERS GO POP CD
NATURAL SINNER
UNITED WE STAND
SPIRIT IN THE SKY
TRAVELLIN' BAND
I CAN'T TELL THE BOTTOM FROM
THE TOP
GOOD MORNING FREEDOM
UP AROUND THE BEND
SHE SOLD ME MAGIC
COME AND GET IT
LOVE OF THE COMMON PEOPLE
SIGNED SEALED DELIVERED
IT'S ALL IN THE GAME
YELLOW RIVER
MY BABY LOVES LOVIN
COTTONFIELDS
LADY D ARBANVILLE

PAPER SLEEVE BOX CD - IMPORT
TINY DANCER
LEVON
RAZOR FACE
MADMAN ACROSS THE WATER
INDIAN SUNSET
HOLIDAY INN

ROTTEN PEACHES
ALL THE NASTIES
GOODBYE
CAPTAIN FANTASTIC AND THE BROWN
DIRT COWBOY
TOWER OF BABEL
BITTER FINGERS
TELL ME WHEN THE WHISTLE BLOWS
SOMEONE SAVED MY LIFE TONIGHT
(GOTTA GET A) MEAL TICKET
BETTER OFF DEAD
WRITING
WE ALL FALL IN LOVE SOMETIMES
CURTAINS
YOUR SONG
I NEED YOU TO TURN TO
TAKE ME TO THE PILOT
NO SHOESTRINGS ON LOUISE
FIRS EPISODE AT HIENTON
SIXTY YEARS ON
BORDER SONG
GREATEST DISCOVERY
CAGE
KING MUST DIE
BAD SIDE OF THE MOON
GREY SEAL

ROCK N ROLL MADONNA
BALLAD OF A WELL-KNOWN GUN
COME DOWN IN TIME
COUNTRY COMFORT
SON OF YOUR FATHER
MY FATHER'S GUN
WHERE TO NOW ST. PETER?
LOVE SONG
AMOREENA
TALKING OLD SOLDIERS
BURN DOWN THE MISSION
INTO THE OLD MAN'S SHOES
MADMAN ACROSS THE WATER
BITCH IS BACK
PINKY
GRIMSBY
DIXIE LILY
SOLAR PRESTIGE A GAMMON
YOU'RE SO STATIC
I'VE SEEN THE SAUCERS
STINKER
DON'T LET THE SUN GO DOWN ON ME
TICKLING
PINBALL WIZARD
SICK CITY
COLD HIGHWAY

STEP INTO CHRISTMAS
FUNERAL FOR A FRIEND
LOVE LIES BLEEDING
CANDLE IN THE WIND
BENNIE AND THE JETS
GOODBYE YELLOW BRICK ROAD
THIS SONG HAS NO TITLE
GREY SEAL
JAMAICA JERK OFF
I'VE SEEN THAT MOVIE TOO
SWEET PAINTED LADY
BALLAD OF DANNY BAILEY (1909-34)
DIRTY LITTLE GIRL
ALL THE GIRLS LOVE ALICE
YOUR SISTER CAN'T TWIST (BUT SHE
CAN ROCK 'N' ROLL)
SATURDAY NIGHT'S ALRIGHT FOR
FIGHTING
ROY ROGERS
SOCIAL DISEASE
HARMONY
DANIEL
TEACHER I NEED YOU
ELDERBERRY WINE
BLUES FOR MY BABY AND ME
MIDNIGHT CREEPER

HAVE MERCY ON THE CRIMINAL
I'M GOING TO BE A TEENAGE IDOL
TEXAN LOVE SONG
CROCODILE ROCK
HIGH-FLYING BIRD
HONKY CAT
MELLOW
I THINK I'M GOING TO KILL MYSELF
SUSIE (DRAMAS)
ROCKET MAN
SALVATION
SLAVE
AMY
MONA LISAS AND MAD HATTERS
HERCULES
TAKE ME TO THE PILOT
HONKY TONK WOMEN
SIXTY YEARS ON
CAN I PUT YOU ON
BAD SIDE OF THE MOON
BURN DOWN THE MISSION
MEDLEY: YELL HELP/ WEDNESDAY
NIGHT/ UGLY
DAN DARE (PILOT OF THE FUTURE)
ISLAND GIRL
GROW SOME FUNK OF YOUR OWN

I FEEL LIKE A BULLET (IN THE GUN OF
ROBERT FORD)
STREET KIDS
HARD LUCK STORY
FEED ME
BILLY BONES AND THE WHITE BIRD
DON'T GO BREAKING MY HEART (DUET
WITH KIKI DEE)
EMPTY SKY
VAL-HALA
WESTERN FOR GATEWAY
HYMN 2000
LADY WHAT'S TOMORROW
SIALS
SCAFFOLD
SKYLINE PIGEON
GUILLVER/ HAY CHEWED/ REPRISE

ROAD TO EL DORADO CD - IMPORT
TOM DICK & HARRY
IT'S HARD TO GO BACK
YOU GOT ANOTHER THOUGHT
TIGHT ROPE
SCARED MAN CAN'T GAMBLE
ALL UP IN IT
FREAK ON THE DANCE FLOOR

THREE LITTLE BIRDS
LOOK BACK
EVERYBODY GONNA

LEGENDARY COVERS CD
COTTONFIELDS
LADY D'ARBANVILLE
I'M A NATURAL SINNER
SPIRIT IN THE SKY
TRAVELLIN' BAND
I CAN'T TELL THE BOTTOM FROM
THE TOP
GOOD MORNING FREEDOM
YOUNG GIFTED AND BLACK
IN THE SUMMERTIME
UP AROUND THE BEND
SHE SOLD ME MAGIC
COME AND GET IT
LOVE OF THE COMMON PEOPLE
SIGNED SEALED DELIVERED I'M YOURS
IT'S ALL IN THE GAME
YELLOW RIVER

**TO RUSSIA WITH ELTON DVD -
IMPORT**
YOUR SON
DANIEL

FUNERAL FOR A FRIEND
PART TIME LOVE
BENNIE AND THE JETS
SIXTY YEARS ON
CANDLE IN THE WIND
BETTER OFF DEAD
ROCKET MAN
I THINK I'M GONNA KILL MYSELF
TONIGHT
MEDLEY: PINBALL WIZARD AND
SATURDAY NIGHT'S ALRIGHT FOR
FIGHTING

CHARTBUSTERS CD
MY BABY LOVES LOVIN'
COTTON FIELDS
LADY D' ARBANVILLE
I'M A NATURAL SINNER
UNITED WE STAND
SPIRIT IN THE SKY
TRAVELIN' BAND
I CAN'T TELL THE BOTTOM FROM
THE TOP
GOOD MORNING FREEDOM
TO BE YOUNG, GIFTED AND BLACK

ELTON JOHN - 25889 CD - IMPORT
BAD SIDE OF THE MOON
AMOREENA
TAKE ME TO THE PILOT
SIXTY YEARS ON
HONKY TONK WOMEN
CAN I PUT YOU ON
BURN DOWN THE MISSION/MY BABY
LEFT ME/GET BACK

ELTON 60: LIVE AT MADISON SQUARE GARDEN DVD THE CONCERT"SIXTY YEARS ON"
MADMAN ACROSS THE WATER
WHERE TO NOW ST. PETER?
HERCULES
BALLAD OF A WELL KNOWN GUN
TAKE ME TO THE PILOT
HIGH FLYING BIRD
HOLIDAY INN
BURN DOWN THE MISSION
BETTER OFF DEAD
LEVON
EMPTY GARDEN (HEY HEY JOHNNY)
HAPPY BIRTHDAY, ELTON (SUNG BY THE AUDIENCE)

DANIEL
HONKY CAT
ROCKET MAN
I GUESS THAT'S WHY THEY CALL IT THE
BLUES
BAND INTRODUCTIONS
THE BRIDGE
ROY ROGERS
MONA LISAS AND MAD HATTERS
SORRY SEEMS TO BE THE HARDEST
WORD
BENNIE AND THE JETS
ALL THE GIRLS LOVE ALICE
TINY DANCER
SOMETHING ABOUT THE WAY YOU
LOOK TONIGHT
PHILADELPHIA FREEDOM
SAD SONGS (SAY SO MUCH)
DON'T LET THE SUN GO DOWN ON ME
I'M STILL STANDING
THE BITCH IS BACK
CROCODILE ROCK
SATURDAY NIGHT'S ALRIGHT FOR
FIGHTING
FUNERAL FOR A FRIEND / LOVES LIES
BLEEDING" (ENCORE)

YOUR SONG" (ENCORE)

**LIVE, RARE & UNSEEN"YOUR SONG"
(ELTON AT 50 MONTAGE)**
BORDER SONG (SWISS TV, 1970)
SIXTY YEARS ON (IN CONCERT, 1970)
TINY DANCER (SOUNDS FOR SATURDAY, 1971)
LEVON (SOUNDS FOR SATURDAY, 1971)
HONKY CAT (ROYAL FESTIVAL HALL, 1972)
ROCKET MAN (ROYAL FESTIVAL HALL, 1972)
CROCODILE ROCK (ROYAL VARIETY SHOW, 1972)
GOODBYE YELLOW BRICK ROAD (TOTP, 1973, LIP-SYNCHED)
DANIEL (EDINBURGH PLAYHOUSE THEATRE, 1976)
SOMEONE SAVED MY LIFE TONIGHT (EDINBURGH PLAYHOUSE THEATRE, 1976)
CANDLE IN THE WIND (EDINBURGH PLAYHOUSE THEATRE, 1976)
I'M STILL STANDING (NIGHT & DAY CONCERT, WEMBLEY, 1984)

SORRY SEEMS TO BE THE HARDEST WORD (EDINBURGH PLAYHOUSE THEATRE, 1976)
BENNIE AND THE JETS (NIGHT & DAY CONCERT, WEMBLEY, 1984)
SONG FOR GUY (THANK YOU AUSTRALIA CONCERT, 1984)
THIS TRAIN DON'T STOP THERE ANYMORE (TOTP, 2001)
TINDERBOX (BBC "IN SESSION", ST. LUKE'S, 2006 - OUTTAKE)
THE BRIDGE (A PORTION OF THE STUDIO VERSION)

ELTON'S NEW YORK STORIES"MONA LISAS AND MAD HATTERS" (ROYAL FESTIVAL HALL, 1972)
WOULDN'T HAVE YOU ANY OTHER WAY (NYC)" (BBC "IN SESSION", ST. LUKE'S, 2006 - OUTTAKE)
EMPTY GARDEN (HEY HEY JOHNNY)" (HAMMERSMITH ODEON, 1982)
WE ALL FALL IN LOVE SOMETIMES/CURTAINS" (MADISON SQUARE GARDEN, 2005)

BELIEVE" (MADISON SQUARE GARDEN, 1995)
BONUS CD (BOX SET ONLY)"SIXTY YEARS ON"
BALLAD OF A WELL KNOWN GUN
WHERE TO NOW ST PETER?
HOLIDAY INN
MADMAN ACROSS THE WATER
LEVON
HERCULES
MONA LISAS AND MAD HATTERS
ROY ROGERS
HIGH FLYING BIRD
BETTER OFF DEAD
EMPTY GARDEN (HEY HEY JOHNNY)
SOMETHING ABOUT THE WAY YOU LOOK TONIGHT
THE BRIDGE
BURN DOWN THE MISSION

MUSE
DRIVING HOME - JOHN
DRIVING TO UNIVERSAL - JOHN
DRIVING TO JACK'S - JOHN
WALK OF SHAME - JOHN
BETTER HAVE A GIFT – JOHN

WRONG GIFT - JOHN
AQUARIUM JOHN -
ARE WE LAUGHING - JOHN
TAKE A WALK WITH ME - JOHN
WHAT SHOULD I DO? - JOHN
BACK TO THE AQUARIUM - JOHN
STEVEN REDECORATES - JOHN
TO THE GUESTHOUSE – JOHN
COOKIE FACTORY - JOHN
MULTIPLE PESONALITY - JOHN
SARAH ESCAPES - JOHN
BACK TO PARAMOUNT - JOHN
MEET CHRISTINE - JOHN
MUSE - JOHN
MUSE [REMIX] – JOHN

**ELTON JOHN & TIM RICE ELTON
JOHN & TIM RICE'S "AIDA"**
ANOTHER PYRAMID - JOHN, RICE
WRITTEN IN THE STARS - JOHN, RICE
EASY AS LIFE [FEATURING ANGELIQUE
KIDJO] - JOHN, RICE
MY STRONGEST SUIT - JOHN, RICE
I KNOW THE TRUTH - JOHN, RICE
NOT ME - JOHN, RICE
AMNERIS' LETTER - JOHN, RICE

STEP TOO FAR JOHN, RICE
LIKE FATHER, LIKE SON - JOHN, RICE
ELABORATE LIVES - JOHN, RICE
HOW I KNOW YOU - JOHN, RICE
MESSENGER - JOHN, RICE
GODS LOVE NUBIA - JOHN, RICE
ENCHANTMENT PASSING THROUGH -
JOHN, RICE
ORCHESTRAL FINALE - RICE

BIG PICTURE

LONG WAY FROM HAPPINESS - JOHN,
TAUPIN
LIVE LIKE HORSES - JOHN, TAUPIN
END WILL COME - JOHN, TAUPIN
IF THE RIVER CAN BEND - JOHN,
TAUPIN
LOVE'S GOT A LOT TO ANSWER FOR -
JOHN, TAUPIN
SOMETHING ABOUT THE WAY YOU
LOOK TONIGHT - JOHN, TAUPIN
BIG PICTURE - JOHN, TAUPIN
RECOVER YOUR SOUL - JOHN, TAUPIN
JANUARY - JOHN, TAUPIN
I CAN'T STEER MY HEART CLEAR OF YOU
- JOHN, TAUPIN

WICKED DREAMS - JOHN, TAUPIN

BREAKING HEARTS
RESTLESS - JOHN, TAUPIN
SLOW DOWN GEORGIE (SHE'S POISON)
- JOHN, TAUPIN
WHO WEARS THESE SHOES? - JOHN,
TAUPIN
BREAKING HEARTS (AIN'T WHAT IT
USED TO BE) - JOHN, TAUPIN
LI'L 'FRIGERATOR - JOHN, TAUPIN
PASSENGERS - JOHN, JOHNSTONE,
TAUPIN, MCHIZE
IN NEON - JOHN, TAUPIN
BURNING BUILDINGS - JOHN, TAUPIN
DID HE SHOOT HER? - JOHN, TAUPIN
SAD SONGS (SAY SO MUCH) - JOHN,
TAUPIN

21 AT 33
CHASING THE CROWN - JOHN, TAUPIN
LITTLE JEANNIE - JOHN, OSBORNE
SARTORIAL ELOQUENCE - JOHN,
ROBINSON
TWO ROOMS AT THE END OF THE
WORLD - JOHN, TAUPIN
DEAR GOD - JOHN, OSBORNE

WHITE LADY WHITE POWDER - JOHN,
TAUPIN
NEVER GONNA FALL IN LOVE AGAIN -
JOHN, ROBINSON
TAKE ME BACK - JOHN, OSBORNE
GIVE ME THE LOVE - JOHN, TZUKE

BLUE MOVES
YOUR STARTER FOR IT - QUAYE
TONIGHT - JOHN, TAUPIN
ONE HORSE TOWN - JOHN, NEWTON-
HOWARD, TAUPIN
CHAMELEON - JOHN, TAUPIN
BOOGIE PILGRIM - JOHN, JOHNSTONE,
QUAYE, TAUPIN
CAGE THE SONGBIRD - JOHN,
JOHNSTONE, TAUPIN
CRAZY WATER - JOHN, TAUPIN
SHOULDER HOLSTER - JOHN, TAUPIN
OUT OF THE BLUE - JOHN, TAUPIN
SORRY SEEMS TO BE THE HARDEST
WORD - JOHN, TAUPIN
BETWEEN SEVENTEEN AND TWENTY -
JOHNSTONE, QUAYE, JOHN, TAUPIN
SOMEONE'S FINAL SONG - JOHN,
TAUPIN

WIDE EYED AND LAUGHING - JOHN,
NEWTON-HOWARD, JOHNSTONE,
QUAYE, TAUPIN
WHERE'S THE SHOORAH? - JOHN,
TAUPIN
IF THERE'S A GOD IN HEAVEN (WHAT'S
HE WAITING FOR?) - JOHN,
JOHNSTONE, TAUPIN
IDOL - JOHN, TAUPIN
THEME FROM A NON-EXISTENT TV
SERIES - JOHN, TAUPIN
BITE YOUR LIP (GET UP AND DANCE!) -
JOHN, JOHNSTONE, QUAYE, TAUPIN

FRIENDS
FRIENDS - JOHN, TAUPIN
HONEY ROLL - JOHN, TAUPIN
THEME (THE FIRST KISS)
SEASONS - JOHN, TAUPIN
VARIATION ON MICHELLE'S SONG (A
DAY IN THE COUNTRY) - JOHN, TAUPIN
CAN I PUT YOU ON - JOHN, TAUPIN
MICHELLE'S SONG - JOHN, TAUPIN
I MEANT TO DO MY WORK TODAY (A
DAY IN THE COUNTRY) - JOHN, TAUPIN
FOUR MOODS BUCKMASTER

SEASONS REPRISE - JOHN, TAUPIN

FIRST VISIT 1971
IT'S ME THAT YOU NEED
YOUR SONG
ROCK ME WHEN HE'S GONE
COME DOWN IN TIME
SKYLINE PIGEON
ROTTEN PEACHES
INDIAN SUNSET
BALLAD OF A WELL-KNOWN GUN
FRIENDS
THE KING MUST DIE
HOLIDAY INN
CAN I PUT YOU ON
COUNTRY COMFORT
HONKY TONK WOMEN
BORDER SONG
MADMAN ACROSS THE WATER
AMOREENA
TAKE ME TO THE PILOT
MY BABY LEFT ME
WHOLE LOTTA SHAKIN' GOING ON

DREAM TICKET
FUNERAL FOR A FRIEND (LOVE LIES
BLEEDING) [DVD]

CANDLE IN THE WIND [DVD]
BENNIE AND THE JETS [DVD]
GOODBYE YELLOW BRICK ROAD [DVD]
SOMEONE SAVED MY LIFE TONIGHT
[DVD]
LITTLE JEANNIE [DVD]
PHILADELPHIA FREEDOM [DVD]
TINY DANCER [DVD]
CAN YOU FEEL THE LOVE TONIGHT?
[DVD]
DANIEL [DVD]
ROCKET MAN (I THINK IT'S GOING TO
BE A LONG, LONG TIME) [DVD]
CLUB AT THE END OF THE STREET
[DVD]
BLUE EYES [DVD]
I GUESS THAT'S WHY THEY CALL IT THE
BLUES [DVD]
THE ONE [DVD]
I DON'T WANNA GO ON WITH YOU LIKE
THAT [DVD]
SACRIFICE [DVD]
SORRY SEEMS TO BE THE HARDEST
WORD [DVD]
COME TOGETHER [DVD]
YOUR SONG [DVD]

SAD SONGS (SAY SO MUCH) [DVD]
I'M STILL STANDING [DVD]
CROCODILE ROCK [DVD]
SATURDAY NIGHT'S ALRIGHT FOR
FIGHTING [DVD]
THE B**** IS BACK [DVD]
DON'T LET THE SUN GO DOWN ON ME
[DVD]
DON'T GO BREAKING MY HEART [DVD]
REHEARSALS/INTERVIEWS [DVD]
SIXTY YEARS ON [DVD]
TAKE ME TO THE PILOT [DVD]
THIS TRAIN DON'T STOP THERE
ANYMORE [DVD]
CARLA ETUDE [DVD]
TONIGHT [DVD]
SORRY SEEMS TO BE THE HARDEST
WORD [DVD]
PHILADELPHIA FREEDOM [DVD]
BURN DOWN THE MISSION [DVD]
DON'T LET THE SUN GO DOWN ON ME
[DVD]
YOUR SONG [DVD]
SATURDAY NIGHT'S ALRIGHT FOR
FIGHTING [DVD]
INTRODUCTION [DVD]

YOUR SONG [DVD]
SOMEONE SAVED MY LIFE TONIGHT
[DVD]
DANIEL [DVD]
MONA LISAS AND MAD HATTERS [DVD]
HONKY CAT [DVD]
ROCKET MAN [DVD]
PHILADELPHIA FREEDOM [DVD]
NIKITA [DVD]
SACRIFICE [DVD]
SORRY SEEMS TO BE THE HARDEST
WORD [DVD]
I GUESS THAT'S WHY THEY CALL IT THE
BLUES [DVD]
THIS TRAIN DON'T STOP THERE
ANYMORE [DVD]
BURN DOWN THE MISSION [DVD]
THE ONE [DVD]
BLUE EYES [DVD]
I'M STILL STANDING [DVD]
CROCODILE ROCK [DVD]
DON'T LET THE SUN GO DOWN ON ME
[DVD]
CIRCLE OF LIFE [DVD]
CANDLE IN THE WIND [DVD]
YOUR SONG [DVD]

ROCKET MAN [DVD]
MONA LISAS AND MAD HATTERS [DVD]
I'M STILL STANDING [DVD]
I GUESS THAT'S WHY THEY CALL IT THE
BLUES [DVD]
EMPTY GARDEN (HEY, HEY JOHNNY)
[DVD]
SACRIFICE [DVD]
CAN YOU FEEL THE LOVE TONIGHT?
[DVD]
BELIEVE [DVD]
I WANT LOVE [DVD]
THIS TRAIN DON'T STOP THERE
ANYMORE [DVD]
ARE YOU READY FOR LOVE [DVD]

PROLOGUE
SATURDAY SUN
SWEET HONESTY
STORMBRINGER
WAY TO BLUE
GO OUT AND GET IT
THE DAY IS DONE
TIME HAS TOLD ME
YOU GET BRIGHTER
THIS MOMENT

I DON'T MIND
PIED PAUPER

A UNIQUE DOUBLE BILL ERIC CLAPTON & HIS BAND, ELTON JOHN & HIS BAND
CROSSROADS
WHITE ROOM
RUN
MISS YOU
TEARING US APART
HOLY MOTHER
IN THE AIR TONIGHT
LAYLA
SUNSHINE OF YOUR LOVE
SHE'S WAITING
WONDERFUL TONIGHT
COCAINE
FOREVER MAN
SORRY SEEMS TO BE THE HARDEST WORD
BLUE EYES/I GUESS THAT'S WHY THEY CALL IT THE BLUES
KISS THE BRIDE
TOO LOW FOR ZERO
I'M STILL STANDING

YOUR SONG
SATURDAY NIGHT'S ALLRIGHT FOR
FIGHTING
GOODBYE YELLOW BRICK ROAD
CROCODILE ROCK
BEATES MEDLEY: I SAW HER STANDING
THERE TWIST/SHOUT/ROCKET MAN
THE B**** IS BACK
DANIEL
DON'T LET THE SUN GO DOWN ON ME
CANDLE IN THE WIND

**ROCKET MAN - NUMBER ONES BY
ELTON JOHN (MAR 27, 2007)**
GOODBYE YELLOW BRICK ROAD
BENNIE AND THE JETS
DANIEL
CROCODILE ROCK
LUCY IN THE SKY WITH DIAMONDS
PHILADELPHIA FREEDOM
ISLAND GIRL
DON'T GO BREAKING MY HEART
SORRY SEEMS TO BE THE HARDEST
WORD
SACRIFICE
DON'T LET THE SUN GO DOWN ON ME

CAN YOU FEEL THE LOVE TONIGHT
YOUR SONG
TINY DANCER
ROCKET MAN (I THINK IT'S GOING TO
BE A LONG, LONG TIME)
CANDLE IN THE WIND
SATURDAY NIGHT'S ALRIGHT (FOR
FIGHTING)

GOOD MORNING TO THE NIGHT BY ELTON VS. PNAU JOHN (2012) - IMPORT
GOOD MORNING TO THE NIGHT
SAD
BLACK ICY STARE
FOREIGN FIELDS
TELEGRAPH TO THE AFTERLIFE
PHOENIX
KARMATRON
SIXTY

GREATEST HITS, VOL. 2 BY ELTON JOHN (1990) - ORIGINAL RECORDING REISSUED BY ELTON JOHN
BITCH IS BACK
LUCY IN THE SKY WITH DIAMONDS

TINY DANCER
I FEEL LIKE A BULLET (IN THE GUN OF
ROBERT FORD)
SOMEONE SAVED MY LIVE TONIGHT
PHILADELPHIA FREEDOM
ISLAND GIRL
GROW SOME FUNK OF YOUR OWN
LEVON
PINBALL WIZARD

RARE MASTERS BY ELTON JOHN (1992)
DISC 1
I'VE BEEN LOVING YOU
HERE'S TO THE NEXT TIME
LADY SAMANTHA
ALL ACROSS THE HAVENS
IT'S ME THAT YOU NEED
JUST LIKE STRANGE RAIN
BAD SIDE OF THE MOON
ROCK AND ROLL MADONNA
GREY SEAL
FRIENDS
MICHELLE'S SONG
SEASONS
VARIATION ON

MICHELLE'S SONG (A DAY IN THE COUNTRY)
CAN I PUT YOU ON
HONEY ROLL
VARIATION ON FRIENDS
ADDITIONAL TRACK INFORMATION
RARE MASTERS SONGS
I MEANT TO DO MY WORK TODAY (A DAY IN THE COUNTRY)
FOUR MOODS
SEASONS REPRISE
DISC 2
MADMAN ACROSS THE WATER
INTO THE OLD MAN'S SHOES
ROCK ME WHEN HE'S GONE
SLAVE
SKYLINE PIGEON
JACK RABBIT
WHENEVER YOU'RE READY (WE'LL GO STEADY AGAIN)
LET ME BE YOUR CAR
SCREW YOU (YOUNG MAN'S BLUES)
STEP INTO CHRISTMAS
HO! HO! HO! WHO'D BE A TURKEY AT CHRISTMAS

EMPTY SKY BY ELTON JOHN (1996) - ORIGINAL RECORDING REISSUED
EMPTY SKY
VAL-HALA
WESTERN FORD GATEWAY
HYMN 2000
LADY WHAT'S TOMORROW
SAILS
SCAFFOLD
SKYLINE PIGEON
GULLIVER / IT'S HAY CHEWED / REPRISE
LADY SAMANTHA
ALL ACROSS THE HAVENS
IT'S ME THAT YOU NEED
JUST LIKE STRANGE RAIN

ELTON JOHN (DLX) (EXP) (DIG) BY ELTON JOHN (2008) - ORIGINAL RECORDING REMASTERED
YOUR SONG
I NEED YOU TO TURN TO
TAKE ME TO THE PILOT
NO SHOES STRINGS ON LOUISE
FIRST EPISODE AT HIENTON
SIXTY YEARS ON
BORDER SONG

THE GREATEST DISCOVERY
THE CAGE
THE KING MUST DIE
YOUR SONG [DEMO VERSION]
I NEED YOU TO TURN TO [PIANO DEMO]
TAKE ME TO THE PILOT [PIANO DEMO]
NO SHOES STRINGS ON LOUISE [PIANO DEMO]
SIXTY YEARS ON [PIANO DEMO]
THE GREATEST DISCOVERY [PIANO DEMO]
THE CAGE [DEMO VERSION]
THE KING MUST DIE [PIANO DEMO]
ROCK 'N' ROLL MADONNA [PIANO DEMO]
THANK YOU MAMA [PIANO DEMO]
ALL THE WAY DOWN TO EL PASO [PIANO DEMO]
I'M GOING HOME [PIANO DEMO]
GREY SEAL [PIANO DEMO]
ROCK AND ROLL MADONNA [INCOMPLETE BAND DEMO]
BAD SIDE OF THE MOON [DEMO VERSION]
GREY SEAL [1970 VERSION]
YOUR SONG [BBC SESSION]

ROCK AND ROLL MADONNA [DEMO VERSION]
BORDER SONG [BBC SESSION (WITH HOOKFOOT)]
TAKE ME TO THE PILOT [BBC SESSION]

1979-87 GREATEST HITS BY ELTON JOHN (2012) - IMPORT

I GUESS THAT'S WHY THEY CALL IT THE BLUES +VIDEO (VIDEO NOT USED IN STORY)
MAMA CAN'T BUY YOU LOVE
LITTLE JEANNIE +VIDEO (VIDEO NOT USED IN STORY)
SAD SONGS (SAY SO MUCH)
I'M STILL STANDING +VIDEO (VIDEO NOT USED IN STORY)
EMPTY GARDEN (HEY, HEY JOHNNY)
HEARTACHE ALL OVER THE WORLD
TOO LOW FOR ZERO
KISS THE BRIDE
BLUE EYES +VIDEO (VIDEO NOT USED IN STORY)
NIKITA +VIDEO (VIDEO NOT USED IN STORY)

WRAP HER UP +VIDEO (VIDEO NOT USED IN STORY)

ONE NIGHT ONLY BY ELTON JOHN (2000) - LIVE

GOODBYE YELLOW BRICK ROAD
PHILADELPHIA FREEDOM
DON'T GO BREAKING MY HEART WITH KIKI DEE
ROCKET MAN (I THINK IT'S GOING TO BE A LONG, LONG TIME)
DANIEL
CROCODILE ROCK
SACRIFICE
CAN YOU FEEL THE LOVE TONIGHT?
BENNIE AND THE JETS
YOUR SONG WITH RONAN KEATING
SAD SONGS (SAY SO MUCH) WITH BRYAN ADAMS
CANDLE IN THE WIND
BITCH IS BACK
SATURDAY NIGHT'S ALRIGHT FOR FIGHTING WITH ANASTACIA
I'M STILL STANDING
I GUESS THAT'S WHY THEY CALL IT THE BLUES

DON'T LET THE SUN GO DOWN ON ME

CLASSIC ELTON JOHN BY ELTON JOHN (1994) - COMPILATION ALL SONGS BY ELTON JOHN AND BERNIE TAUPIN

TAKE ME TO THE PILOT
BURN DOWN THE MISSION
FRIENDS
SATURDAY NIGHT'S ALRIGHT FOR FIGHTING FEAT. COLIN WOODSIDE
MADMAN ACROSS THE WATER ALTERNATE VERSION THAT APPEARS ON RARE MASTERS
TINY DANCER
HONKY CAT
CROCODILE ROCK
MONA LISAS AND MAD HATTERS
LEVON
BROKEBACK MOUNTAIN FEAT. SIMON BLACK

CAPTAIN FANTASTIC BY ELTON JOHN (2004) - HYBRID SACD - DSD

CAPTAIN FANTASTIC AND THE BROWN DIRT COWBOY
TOWER OF BABEL

BITTER FINGERS
TELL ME WHEN THE WHISTLE BLOWS
SOMEONE SAVED MY LIFE TONIGHT
MEAL TICKET, (GOTTA GET A)
BETTER OFF DEAD
WRITING
WE ALL FALL IN LOVE SOMETIMES
CURTAINS
LUCY IN THE SKY WITH DIAMONDS
ONE DAY AT A TIME
PHILADELPHIA FREEDOM

CHRONICLES (LONG) BY ELTON JOHN (2005) - BOX SET
DISC 1

YOUR SONG
I NEED YOU TO TURN TO
TAKE ME TO THE PILOT
NO SHOE STRINGS ON LOUISE
FIRST EPISODE AT HIENTON
SIXTY YEARS ON
BORDER SONG
GREATEST DISCOVERY
CAGE
KING MUST DIE
BAD SIDE OF THE MOON

GREY SEAL
ROCK 'N' ROLL MADONNA
DISC 2
BALLAD OF A WELL-KNOWN GUN
COME DOWN IN TIME
COUNTRY COMFORT
SON OF YOUR FATHER
MY FATHER'S GUN
WHERE TO NOW ST. PETER?
LOVE SONG
AMOREENA
TALKING OLD SOLDIERS
BURN DOWN THE MISSION
INTO THE OLD MAN'S SHOES
MADMAN ACROSS THE WATER WITH
MICK RONSON
DISC 3
TINY DANCER
LEVON
RAZOR FACE
MADMAN ACROSS THE WATER
INDIAN SUNSET
HOLIDAY INN
ROTTEN PEACHES
ALL THE NASTIES
GOODBYE

ELTON JOHN'S CHRISTMAS PARTY
BY ELTON JOHN (2006)
STEP INTO CHRISTMAS
FELIZ NAVIDAD
MAN WITH ALL THE TOYS
CHANGE AT CHRISTMAS, A (SAY IT ISN'T SO)
IT DOESN'T OFTEN SNOW AT CHRISTMAS
SPOTLIGHT ON CHRISTMAS
JINGLE BELL ROCK
RUN RUDOLPH RUN
MERRY CHRISTMAS BABY
CHRISTMAS ISLAND
CHRISTMAS MUST BE TONIGHT
2000 MILES
DECEMBER WILL BE MAGIC AGAIN
NEW YEAR'S DAY
CALLING IT CHRISTMAS

ELTON JOHN AT THE VERONA ARENA: 3CD
DISC ONE
FUNERAL / LOVE LIES
SATURDAY NIGHT
BURN DOWN THE MISSION

GOODBYE YELLOW BRICK ROAD
BLUES
DANIEL
HONKY CAT
I WANT LOVE
ROCKET MAN
SAD SONGS
PILOT
DISC TWO
SORRY
TINY DANCER
SACRIFICE
DON'T LET THE SUN GO DOWN ON ME
ALL THE YOUNG GIRLS LOVE ALICE
CANDLE IN THE WIND
SKYLINE PIGEON
ARE YOU READY FOR LOVE
BENNIE
BITCH IS BACK
CROCODILE ROCK
I'M STILL STANDING
YOUR SONG
DISC THREE
EXCLUSIVE PHOTOS FROM THE NIGHT
(NOT USED IN THE STORY)

PICKIN' ON ELTON JOHN BY PICKIN' ON ELTON JOHN (2001) - ORIGINAL RECORDING REISSUED

SORRY SEEMS TO BE THE HARDEST WORD PICKIN' ON (PICKIN' ON NOT USED IN STORY)

DANIEL PICKIN' ON

GOODBYE YELLOW BRICK ROAD PICKIN' ON (PICKIN' ON NOT USED IN STORY)

TAKE ME TO THE PILOTPICKIN' ON (PICKIN' ON NOT USED IN STORY)

BENNIE AND THE JETS PICKIN' ON

ROCKET MAN PICKIN' ON

YOUR SONG PICKIN' ON (PICKIN' ON NOT USED IN STORY)

ISLAND GIRL PICKIN' ON

LUCY IN THE SKY WITH DIAMONDS PICKIN' ON

SOMEONE SAVED MY LIFE TONIGHT PICKIN' ON (PICKIN' ON NOT USED IN STORY)

WHERE TO NOW ST. PETER? PICKIN' ON (PICKIN' ON NOT USED IN STORY)

CROCODILE ROCK PICKIN' ON (PICKIN' ON NOT USED IN STORY)

CANDLE IN THE WIND PICKIN' ON
(PICKIN' ON NOT USED IN STORY)
DON'T LET THE SUN GO DOWN ON ME
PICKIN' ON (PICKIN' ON NOT USED IN
STORY)

ELTON JOHN - RECOVER YOUR SOUL PT.2
RECOVER YOUR SOUL
BIG MAN IN A LITTLE SUIT
I KNOW WHY I'M IN LOVE
RECOVER YOUR SOUL

ELTON JOHN - LIVE IN BARCELONA BY ELTON JOHN (2002) - COLOR
DON'T LET THE SUN GO DOWN ON ME
I'M STILL STANDING
I GUESS THAT'S WHY THEY CALL IT THE
BLUES
TINY DANCER
PHILADELPHIA FREEDOM
BURN DOWN THE MISSION
SIMPLE LIFE
THE ONE
I DON'T WANNA GO ON WITH YOU LIKE
THAT
MONA LISAS AND MAD HATTERS

SORRY SEEMS TO BE THE HARDEST
WORD
DANIEL
BLUE AVENUE
THE LAST SONG
FUNERAL FOR A FRIEND"/"LOVE LIES
BLEEDING
SAD SONGS (SAY SO MUCH)
THE SHOW MUST GO ON
SATURDAY NIGHT'S ALRIGHT (FOR
FIGHTING)
SACRIFICE
SONG FOR GUY"/"YOUR SONG

CHARTBUSTERS GO POP BY ELTON JOHN (1999)
NATURAL SINNER
UNITED WE STAND
SPIRIT IN THE SKY
TRAVELLIN' BAND
GOOD MORNING FREEDOM
I CAN'T TELL THE BOTTOM FROM THE
TOP
UP AROUND THE BEND
SHE SOLD ME MAGIC
COME AND GET IT

LOVE OF THE COMMON PEOPLE
SIGNED SEALED DELIVERED
IT'S ALL IN THE GAME
YELLOW RIVER
MY BABY LOVES LOVIN
COTTONFIELDS
LADY D ARBANVILLE

IF THE RIVER CAN BEND BY ELTON JOHN (1998) – IMPORT
CD 1
IF THE RIVER CAN BEND (EDIT)
BENNIE & THE JETS
SATURDAY NIGHT'S ALRIGHT FOR FIGHTING
IF THE RIVER CAN BEND
CD 2
IF THE RIVER CAN BEND (EDIT)
DON'T LET THE SUN GO DOWN ON ME - LIVE
I GUESS THAT'S WHY THEY CALL IT THE BLUES - LIVE
SORRY SEEMS TO BE THE HARDEST WORD - LIVE

THE PIANO MEN- LIVE IN TOKYO BY ELTON JOHN AND BILLY JOEL (2009) – IMPORT

ELTON JOHN & BILLY JOEL

YOUR SONG

DON'T LET THE SUN GO DOWN ON ME

BILLY JOEL

ANGRY YOUNG MAN

THE STRANGER

JUST THE WAY YOU ARE

ALLENTOWN

I GO TO EXTREMES

ELTON JOHN & BILLY JOEL

MY LIFE

BILLY JOEL

THE RIVER OF DREAMS

CANDLE IN THE WIND

IT'S STILL ROCK AND ROLL TO ME

BIG SHOT

ELTON JOHN & BILLY JOEL

THE BITCH IS BACK

YOU MAY BE RIGHT

PIANO MAN

ARE YOU READY FOR LOVE BY ELTON JOHN (2003) – IMPORT

ARE YOU READY FOR LOVE
ARE YOU READY FOR LOVE
THREE WAY LOVE AFFAIR

CELEBRATING ELTON JOHN'S 50TH BIRTHDAY MARCH 25, 1997 BY ELTON JOHN (1997) - CD

YOUR SONG
BURN DOWN THE MISSION
LEVON
ROCKET MAN
BENNIE AND THE JETS
SOMEONE SAVED MY LIFE TONIGHT
ISLAND GIRL
BLUE EYES
SAD SONGS (SAY SO MUCH)
THE ONE
BELIEVE
YOU CAN MAKE HISTORY (YOUNG AGAIN)

STRING QUARTET TRIBUTE TO ELTON JOHN SONGS

SAD SONGS (SAY SO MUCH)
BENNIE AND THE JETS

I'M STANDING STILL
TINY DANCER
GOODBYE ENGLAND'S ROSE AKA
"CANDLE IN THE WIND"
LITTLE JEANNIE
ISLAND GIRL
I GUESS THAT'S WHY THEY CALL IT THE
BLUES
GOODBYE YELLOW BRICK ROAD
YOUR SONG VERSION FROM THE
LUHRMANN FILM MOULIN ROUGE
BITCH IS BACK
BELIEVE
BLESSED
CAPTAIN & ME, FOR STRING QUARTET

**ORIGINAL SIN BY ELTON JOHN
(2002) - IMPORT**
ORIGINAL SIN PT. 1
ORIGINAL SIN
IM STILL STANDING LIVE
THIS TRAIN DONT STOP THERE
ANYMORE LIVE
THIS TRAIN DONT STOP THERE
ANYMORE (VIDEO)

ORIGINAL SIN PT. 2
ORIGINAL SIN
ORIGINAL SIN
ALL THE GIRLS LOVE ALICE
ORIGINAL SIN #2
ENTRE PAREDES
ENTREGATE
SE OLVIDO
CELOS
SIN TI
TE DARE
YING YANG TU
HIJO MACHO
TIERRA
CORONA
VIVE
EN SUS OJOS

**ELTON JOHN SONGBOOK BY ELTON
TRIBUTE: JOHN (1996)**
CANDLE IN THE WIND
CAN YOU FEEL THE LOVE TONIGHT
BENNIE & THE YETS
SOMETHING ABOUT THE WAY YOU
LOOK TONIGHT
DANIEL

I GUESS THAT'S WHY THEY CALL THE
BLUES
I JUST CAN'T WAIT TO BE KING
SONG FOR GUY
I'M STILL STANDING
HONKY CAT
RECOVER YOU SOUL
LEVON
DON'T GO BREAKING MY HEART
RETURN TO PARADISE
LITTLE JEANIE
YOUR SONG

RUNAWAY TRAIN BY ELTON JOHN AND ERIC CLAPTON (1992) - SINGLE

RUNAWAY TRAIN - ELTON JOHN & ERIC
CLAPTON
THROUGH THE STORM - ELTON JOHN &
ARETHA FRANKLIN
DON'T LET THE SUN GO DOWN ON ME -
ELTON JOHN & GEORGE MICHAEL
SLOW RIVERS - ELTON JOHN & CLIFF
RICHARD

REG DWIGHT'S PIANO GOES POP BY ELTON JOHN - IMPORT

MY BABY LOVES LOVE
COTTONFIELDS
LADY D'ARBANVILLE
NATURAL SINNER
UNITED WE STAND
SPIRIT IN THE SKY
TRAVELLIN' BAND
I CAN'T TELL THE TOP FROM THE BOTTOM
GOOD MORNING FREEDOM
YOUNG GIFTED & BLACK
IN THE SUMMERTIME
UP AROUND THE BEND
SNAKE IN THE GRASS
NEANDERTHAL MAN
YOUNG, GIFTED AND BLACK
COME AND GET IT
LOVE OF THE COMMON PEOPLE
SIGNED SEALED AND DELIVERED

VISA GOLD PRESENTS ELTON JOHN'S GOLD BY ELTON JOHN (1995) - CD
YOUR SONG
SOMEONE SAVED MY LIFE TONIGHT
PHILADELPHIA FREEDOM
COME DOWN IN TIME
ROCKET MAN (I THINK IT'S GOING TO BE A LONG LONG TIME)
HONKY CAT
I GUESS THAT'S WHY THEY CALL IT THE BLUES
SAD SONGS (SAY SO MUCH)
SORRY SEEMS TO BE THE HARDEST WORD
I'M STILL STANDING
THE BITCH IS BACK
SATURDAY NIGHT'S ALRIGHT (FOR FIGHTING)

RECOVER YOUR SOUL BY ELTON JOHN (1998) - SINGLE
RECOVER YOUR SOUL
KNOW WHY I'M IN LOVE

BIBLIOGRAPHY

THE FOLLOWING TITLES WERE FOUND
ON:
http://www.cduniverse.com/search/xx/m
usic/artist/Elton+John/a/albums.htmCarib
ou CD
GOODBYE YELLOW BRICK ROAD CD
LOVE SONGS CD
ELTON JOHN CD
UNION CD
GREATEST HITS DEFINITIVE ALBUM
1970-2002 CD
GREATEST HITS CD
TUMBLEWEED CONNECTION CD
GREATEST HITS 1970-2002 CD
CAPTAIN FANTASTIC AND THE BROWN
DIRT COWBOY CD
ROCKET MAN: THE DEFINITIVE HITS CD
– IMPORT
TOO LOW FOR ZERO CD
MADMAN ACROSS THE WATER CD
CARIBOU CD
ELTON JOHN - 11-17-70 CD
LIVE IN AUSTRALIA CD
FOX CD

HONKY CHATEAU CD
SINGLE MAN CD
JUMP UP CD
TWO ROOMS: CELEBRATING THE SONGS
OF ELTON JOHN & BERNIE TAUPIN. CD
ELTON JOHN / BERNIE TAUPIN -
TRIBUTE TO JOHN, ELTON / TAUPIN,
BERNIE
DON'T SHOOT ME I'M ONLY THE PIANO
PLAYER CD
COMPLETE THOM BELL SESSIONS CD
SLEEPING WITH THE PAST CD
ICE ON FIRE CD
REG STRIKES BACK CD
REG STRIKES BACK CD (3 DISC)
MADE IN ENGLAND CD
ROCK OF THE WESTIES CD
CAPTAIN & THE KID CD
GREATEST HITS 1976-1986 CD
PEACHTREE ROAD: SPECIAL
COLLECTOR'S EDITION CD
GREATEST HITS/ONE NIGHT ONLY:
DELUXE SOUND & VISION (DVD/PAL-0)
CD
VICTIM OF LOVE CD
TWO ROOMS-CELEBRATING DVD

INSTRUMENTAL MEMORIES CD –
IMPORT
DUETS CD
LEGENDARY COVERS AS SUNG BY ELTON
JOHN CD
GREATEST HITS VOL. 3 CD
HERE & THERE CD – IMPORT
RED PIANO TOUR CD
ELTON JOHN - 25889 CD – IMPORT
THE ONE CD
GOODBYE YELLOW BRICK ROAD (MINI
LP SLEEVE) CD
SONGS FROM THE WEST COAST CD
VERY BEST OF ELTON JOHN CD
16 LEGENDARY COVERS FROM 1969-70
CD
TO BE CONTINUED... CD
LADY SAMANTHA CD
LEATHER JACKETS CD
CHARTBUSTERS GO POP CD
PAPER SLEEVE BOX CD – IMPORT
ROAD TO EL DORADO CD – IMPORT
LEGENDARY COVERS CD
TO RUSSIA WITH ELTON DVD – IMPORT
CHARTBUSTERS CD

ELTON 60: LIVE AT MADISON SQUARE
GARDEN DVD

ROCKET MAN - NUMBER ONES BY ELTON
JOHN (MAR 27, 2007)

GOOD MORNING TO THE NIGHT BY
ELTON VS. PNAU JOHN (2012) – IMPORT

GREATEST HITS, VOL. 2 BY ELTON JOHN
(1990) - ORIGINAL RECORDING
REISSUED BY ELTON JOHN

RARE MASTERS BY ELTON JOHN (1992)

EMPTY SKY BY ELTON JOHN (1996) -
ORIGINAL RECORDING REISSUED

1979-87 GREATEST HITS BY ELTON
JOHN (2012) - IMPORT

ONE NIGHT ONLY BY ELTON JOHN
(2000) – LIVE

CAPTAIN FANTASTIC BY ELTON JOHN
(2004) - HYBRID SACD - DSD

CHRONICLES (LONG) BY ELTON JOHN
(2005) - BOX SET

ELTON JOHN'S CHRISTMAS PARTY BY
ELTON JOHN (2006)

PICKIN' ON ELTON JOHN BY PICKIN' ON
ELTON JOHN (2001) - ORIGINAL
RECORDING REISSUED

RECOVER YOUR SOUL BY ELTON JOHN (1998) – SINGLE
ELTON JOHN - RECOVER YOUR SOUL PT.2
ARE YOU READY FOR LOVE BY ELTON JOHN (2003) – IMPORT
STRING QUARTET TRIBUTE TO ELTON JOHN SONGS
ORIGINAL SIN BY ELTON JOHN (2002) – IMPORT PARTS ONE AND TWO
ORIGINAL SIN #2 (FOREIGN VERSION)
ELTON JOHN SONGBOOK BY ELTON TRIBUTE: JOHN (1996)

THE FOLLOWING TITLES WERE FOUND ON:
http://www.starpulse.com/Music/John,_El ton/Discography/
ELTON JOHN & TIM RICE ELTON JOHN & TIM RICE'S "AIDA"
MUSE
BIG PICTURE
BREAKING HEARTS
21 AT 33
BLUE MOVES
FRIENDS

THE FOLLOWING TITLES WERE FOUND ON:
http://www.mtv.com/music/artist/john_elton/albums.jhtml
FIRST VISIT 1971
DREAM TICKET
PROLOGUE
A UNIQUE DOUBLE BILL ERIC CLAPTON & HIS BAND, ELTON JOHN & HIS BAND
ELTON JOHN (DLX) (EXP) (DIG) BY ELTON JOHN (2008) - ORIGINAL RECORDING REMASTERED
http://www.artistdirect.com/nad/store/artist/album/0,,4685315,00.html

CLASSIC ELTON JOHN BY ELTON JOHN (1994) - COMPILATION
http://en.wikipedia.org/wiki/Classic_Elton_John

ELTON JOHN AT THE VERONA ARENA: 3CD
http://hmv.com/hmvweb/displayProductDetails.do?sku=800270#anchorSpecialFeatures

ELTON JOHN - LIVE IN BARCELONA BY ELTON JOHN (2002) – COLOR
http://en.wikipedia.org/wiki/Live_in_Barcelona_(Elton_John_DVD)

IF THE RIVER CAN BEND BY ELTON JOHN (1998) – IMPORT
http://eil.com/shop/moreinfo.asp?catalogid=122412

REG DWIGHT'S PIANO GOES POP BY ELTON JOHN – IMPORT
http://www.last.fm/music/Elton+John/Reg+Dwight's+Piano+Goes+Pop

THE PIANO MEN- LIVE IN TOKYO BY ELTON JOHN AND BILLY JOEL (2009) – IMPORT
http://newreleases.fullalbums.org/blogs/2010/11/28/elton-john-the-piano-men-live-in-tokyo-elton-john-billy-joel-2009

CELEBRATING ELTON JOHN'S 50TH BIRTHDAY MARCH 25, 1997 BY ELTON JOHN (1997) - CD
http://www.fotrecords.com/index.php?cmd=products&prod_id=9096

RUNAWAY TRAIN BY ELTON JOHN AND ERIC CLAPTON (1992) - SINGLE
http://www.discogs.com/Elton-John-Eric-Clapton-Runaway-Train/release/1258121

VISA GOLD PRESENTS ELTON JOHN'S GOLD BY ELTON JOHN (1995) - CD
http://www.boudnik.org/~cos/music/EltonJohn/visa_gold.html

ABOUT THE AUTHOR

I was 59 years old; a mother of three very special and supportive adult children and a grandmother of three wonderful grandsons (I now have five grandchildren.) when I started writing my first book whilst watching a Bon Jovi concert DVD. (I am an avid fan, if you can call me that; crazy is more like it.)

I write from the heart and I really enjoyed writing the book so I wrote another using a different artist, and the books kept coming to me and I kept writing them.(with a little help from above)

Because I use different artist/artists song titles I have to be very careful with Copyright so a lot of legal requirements have to be taken into consideration before publishing the books. I also needed a name that would connect my books to each other; so the "Song Title Series" books began.

All my books are short stories; however it depends on how many song titles there are to be used, as to the length of the book. Some artists didn't have enough song titles on their own so I combined them with a few other artists. Other artists had that many song titles that I could have written a novel; but it would have ended up being boring.

Challenges I like, so writing books with various artists are a lot of fun and require careful thinking.

Why should I have all the fun writing the books and not be able to share them with everyone; so I have converted them into large print books so that you can share my fun as well.

Hopefully in the not too distant future; the books will also be available as audio books so that no-one will miss out on my fun and enjoyment of writing these unique books. I hope that you enjoy reading them.

My web site www.songtitleseries.com is the place to visit for updates of new books and a place to purchase other titles in other formats.

OTHER BOOKS IN THE SONG TITLE SERIES

Bon Jovi – Wanted Dead Or Alive
Green Day
AC/DC
Beach Boys
Slim Dusty
Country Women
Five Country Men
Six Crooners
Three Crooners
ABBA
The Rat Pack
Elton John
Classic 50s & 60s Rock 'N' Roll

TESTIMONIALS

Joan Maguire Books are very nice, I enjoy reading them so much, they are hard to put down!! Especially when she does one about Bonjovi and their songs!!! If I can say, it is worth every penny, when you buy one!!! The Books make nice presents, for a person whom loves to read!!! I can guarantee that you will LOVE these books, because I do!!!!!!!!! Dawn from Newark, Delaware in the United States of America

I am Susie and would like to tell you guys, how much I am enjoying Joan Maguire's Books!! They are very enjoyable, and they are something that you do not ever want to put down!! I really enjoy these books; I can't wait until the next one that she puts out!!!!!!! I say go to your local book store, today and get one, you will not be disappointed!!!!! Sue-from the United States of America

After reading through your range of books I felt I must compliment you Joan on the imaginative and entertaining way in which you presented each group and the Musicians in those groups. The way the stories were constructed is a credit to your work ethic. These must have taken considerable time to piece together and it is obviously a work of love for you.

I wish you all the success you truly deserve and look forward to seeing you next time you visit Tamworth.

Peter Harkins
Managing Director Cheapa Music
Country Music Capital Tamworth

The song titles series are books that were intriguing and were hard to believe that these short stories were written within the incorporated song titles of the artists that are mentioned in the titles. I loved what I have read so far and think that anyone with an imagination and love of music as the author you will surely enjoy reading these.

L.K. Brisbane Australia.